Maya Blake's hopes of becoming a writer were born when she picked up her first romance at thirteen. Little did she know her dream would come true! Does she still pinch herself every now and then to make sure it's not a dream? Yes, she does! Feel free to pinch her, too, via Twitter, Facebook or Goodreads! Happy reading!

KIDNAPPED FOR HIS ROYAL HEIR

MAYA BLAKE

MILLS & BOON

First Published in Great Britain 2020
by Mills & Boon, an imprint of HarperCollins*Publishers*
1 London Bridge Street, London, SE1 9GF

© 2020 Maya Blake

ISBN: 978-0-263-08728-4

MIX
Paper from
responsible sources
FSC™ C007454

This book is produced from independently certified FSC™ paper
to ensure responsible forest management.
For more information visit www.harpercollins.co.uk/green.

Printed and bound in Great Britain
by CPI Group (UK) Ltd, Croydon, CR0 4YY

CHAPTER ONE

VIOLET BARRINGHALL HELD the thick envelope in her hand, mutiny brimming in her heart. She managed to dredge up a thin smile for the smartly dressed courier before shutting her apartment door.

She knew its sender without peeking inside. Its weighted richness shrieked wealth, and its creamy, seamless perfection stressed its importance. The gold-embossed emblem on the top right-hand corner was distinctive enough without her years-long exposure to the family that bore it with centuries-old pride and unapologetic arrogance.

But more than that she encountered an even purer strain of that pride and arrogance on a daily basis in the form of His Royal Highness Prince Zakary Philippe Montegova—the sender of the envelope in her hand.

It wasn't a highbrow invitation.

No, this was a *summons*.

She knew this because she'd been responsible for sending out *those* invitations for his latest fundraising event herself, in her role as his long-suffering dogsbody for the last twelve weeks.

Three months, and counting, of pure hell. Of relentless commands and impossible expectations of perfection from a man—no, a *prince*—who demanded the very best of himself and therefore of everyone else around him as well.

As Director of the House of Montegova Trust, a foundation that dealt with everything from managing Montegovan business interests abroad to charity and conservation work all over the world, the trust had gained international acclaim for the small but immensely wealthy Mediterranean kingdom.

Together with his brother, Crown Prince Remi Montegova, and their mother, the Queen, Zak had elevated the status of the kingdom to even greater heights since the untimely death of the King over a decade ago.

Where others would've grown content at achieving multi-billionaire status, unquestioning respect and reverence, and rested on their laurels, Zak was even more driven, his terrifying, breakneck work ethic inexhaustible. Heck, every facet of his *life* was lived in high octane.

Right down to the revolving-door speed of his personal liaisons.

Violet didn't want to think about that. Right now, she'd give anything to completely erase Zak Montegova from her memory. At least for the next twelve hours.

But she couldn't.

She'd committed to being at his beck and call. In fact, that clause was specifically stated in her contract with the trust. While she had several reservations about the man himself, she couldn't forget that her degree in community development and her personal career ambition as a conservationist would be given a huge boost with a stint at the trust on her CV. It was why her deliberations about accepting the secondment offer in New York had been woefully short but immensely painful.

Because, aside from her grimace-inducing personal history with Zak, it directly played into her mother's blatant and conniving plans.

Despite telling herself *that incident* was a thing of the past, Violet hadn't been able to consign it to history. Like a recurring nightmare, it leapt to life and replayed in vivid Technicolor every time she was in Zak's presence, which these days happened to be several hours of every day.

Three more months. A mere ninety-odd days. What could possibly go wrong?

Like an impossibly perfect spectre, his face loomed in her mind's eye.

Formidable perfection. Insufferably handsome, with a royal swagger that shouted his awareness of his charisma. The raw prowess she'd heard whispers about long before she'd first encountered him.

Every dismissive word he'd thrown at her that day in her mother's garden six years ago had been steeped in pure masculine arrogance. He'd carried that entitlement in his thick, broad shoulders and arrogant slant of his head as he'd walked away, secure in the knowledge that his manhood was assured, even worshipped by yet another woman, while he'd cruelly rebuffed the attention he'd garnered.

Violet's face heated up at the memory. Her hand curled tighter around the envelope, one heartbeat away from crumpling the expensive paper. Slowly, she unclenched her fist, breathed deeply to restore her equilibrium. She wasn't eighteen any more, hadn't been for six long, tough years.

She'd had to grow up pretty damned fast shortly after that eye-opening party, thanks to an unexpected heart attack taking her father, and the discovery that the life of luxury they'd led had been lived on the back of a ruthlessly guarded facade of falsehoods, humiliating ingratiation and a blatant and ultimately futile exercise of robbing Peter to pay Paul.

The shocking revelation that the Earl and Countess Barringhall weren't as esteemed or as wealthy as they'd led the world to believe, that they were in fact destitute to the point of bankruptcy, had become an open, humiliating secret. Even far away at university, Violet had been subjected to snide and cruel gossip, social media playing its part in serialising the true status of her family to the world.

It was why Violet had buried herself in her work at the International Conservation Trust. And when the opportunity came up to work away from Barringhall and her mother's ever-increasing efforts to marry her off to someone socially advantageous, Violet had grabbed it with both hands and taken the position in Oxford.

But with senior positions in the field going to more experienced colleagues, not conservationists with less than two years' experience, she'd known it was only prudent to redouble her efforts to accelerate her career path and put herself entirely out of her mother's orbit.

She'd taken this job despite knowing her mother's close friendship with the Queen of Montegova would be exploited to the utmost in her bid to marry her daughter off.

Violet had considered telling her mother not to bother because she wouldn't succeed. Little did her mother know that Zak Montegova couldn't have made his feelings for Violet any clearer than he had that night six years ago or during the last few weeks she'd been working alongside him.

To Zak, she barely existed.

So she didn't understand why this envelope had been delivered here, now. After ten hours' exposure to His Royal High-Handedness today, she'd hoped for a night's reprieve before being subjected to his disturbing presence again.

Lips pressed together to hold her feelings inside, she slid a finger beneath the flap.

The note was brief. Succinct. *Imperious.*

My assistant has been taken ill. You will take her place in accompanying me to the Conservation Society fundraiser, which starts in an hour. A chauffeur is at your disposal.

    Don't let me down.
HRHZ

The inherent threat in those four final words had kept her awake for more nights in the past three months than anything else had done in her whole life.

That need for her to be exemplary in all things lest the stain of gossip, that underlying suspicion that she was a freeloader, a *leech*, because of her parents' infamous misdeeds, attach itself to her. So far it'd proved an uphill battle, social media and her mother's relentless pursuit of status playing their part in keeping the gossip mill alive and robust.

But she only needed to withstand this for a while longer, to *earn* her place in life through hard work and dedication to her chosen career. Prove sceptics like Zakary Montegova wrong. If that included stepping into his assistant's shoes for one night...

She could gain invaluable experience from other conservationists attending the much-vaunted and anticipated event. So why were thoughts of Zak uppermost in her brain? Why was her heart hammering at the prospect of seeing him again?

She jumped when her phone rang from where it lay on the tiny console table next to the front door. Her Greenwich Village apartment was compact enough to cross in a handful of steps, although she suspected who it was before she reached for the phone. Sure enough, the cynical *HRH* she'd programmed into the contacts was displayed in green.

'Hello?'

'You have received my note, yes?'

She hated it that her fingers shook at the deep, faintly accented tones that blended Italian, French and Spanish in an enthralling mix that made up Montegova's language and history.

'Since you informed the courier to hand it over personally, no doubt you've been told exactly that. And good evening, to you too. Your Highness.' She couldn't stem the snippiness from her voice even as she grew irritated with herself for letting him get under her skin. For this heart-banging-against-ribs effect he so effortlessly commanded from her.

But hadn't he done that to her since she'd first set eyes on him at twelve? Hadn't she and her twin sister, Sage, watched him that first time from their bedroom window? Hadn't Violet, freshly done with reading her favourite fairy tale, instantly placed herself in the Princess's shoes, with Zakary Montegova in the leading role of Prince Charming, because in that seemingly serendipitous moment when he'd looked up and locked eyes with her, he'd been her every wish come to life? The answer to those desperate, seemingly futile prayers for deliverance from her parents' endless arguments, the whispers and conversations that suddenly stopped when she and her sisters walked into the room, and their mother's constant badgering about making strategic friendships?

She'd hated herself for that weak moment later, of course. Because books were books. Nothing in real life could mislead her into thinking she needed a boy...or man...to save her. That the answer to her self-worth lay in a prince whose gaze turned cool and dismissive as he stared at her from across the top of his perfectly polished sports car.

His Perfect Highness didn't immediately respond to her snippiness now, and that drawn-out extra second tightened Violet's already strung-out nerves. He'd always had a knack for making her feel self-conscious, even awkward once upon a time.

But only if you give him that power.

Where she would've rushed into further speech at twelve or eighteen, Violet forced herself to hold her tongue now. To wait him out. As if her heart wasn't banging harder just from the sound of his voice. As if her palms weren't growing clammy, reminding her how she'd *ruffled* him, for a very brief, blink-and-you'll-miss-it instant, six years ago.

It was infuriating that her brain refused to let go of that

moment, the scent and, sweet heaven, the *taste* of him still lingering, vivid and real and *affecting*, after all this time.

'Personal dealings with couriers are outside my remit, so you'll have to excuse my ignorance,' Prince Zakary drawled, dragging her attention back to the present. Back to his exclusive importance. To the reminder that he dealt with heads of state and *Fortune 500* CEOs, not the common working class. 'But I'm pleased to note the urgency of the situation was relayed. I trust you're ready?'

'No, I'm not. I received the note five minutes ago. I haven't even thought about what I'm going to wear yet.'

'Think fast, then, Violet. I'll be at your apartment in twenty minutes.'

'What? You said I had an hour before your chauffeur fetched me.'

'There's been a change of plan, which necessitated this call. My foreign minister wishes to meet with me before the fundraiser starts.'

'And what does that have to do with me?'

Again, he paused for an extra beat. 'Since you're acting as my assistant, your presence is also required at the meeting. Unless you feel you're not up to the task…?'

That barely veiled insinuation stung.

'Not that long ago I spent three weeks under an intense sun, with very little sleep, cleaning and tagging hundreds of birds after an oil tanker spilled its contents on the other side of the world, Your Highness. I'm sure I'm up to *taking notes* at a meeting. Unless you'll be conducting it in something other than one of the five languages I speak fluently?' That need to prove her worth to him, to ram her few but much prideful accomplishments down his throat, grated for a moment before she owned it.

She'd learned to her cost that *timid* didn't work with Zak.

Anything other than toe-to-toe combat was just asking to be eaten alive and spat aside with singeing indifference. He responded to challenges, usually attempted by misguided fools who dared to say no to him. But occasionally it didn't hurt to remind the man that simply because that word didn't exist in his vocabulary, it didn't mean she intended to gushingly enquire *how high* when he said *jump*.

'I'm well aware of the contents of your résumé, Lady Barringhall. You don't need to recite it to me, especially not when time is of the essence.'

'Of course not. Your Highness. Just as I won't remind you that you're the one who called me. That you're the one wasting time by keeping me on the phone when I could be getting dressed.'

'Ah.' His voice was a cool, deep exhalation. 'I imagined you were an expert at multi-tasking. Since I don't recall that listed as one of your accomplishments, I'll have to make my own judgement on that score. You now have fifteen minutes, Lady Barringhall.'

The line went dead, and Violet couldn't stop the uncouth word that erupted from her lips. That little catharsis freed a layer of tension and propelled her to her tiny bedroom, where she rummaged through her meagre wardrobe in search of the gown she hadn't worn since her twenty-first.

Recalling how different that birthday had been from her eighteenth, she pursed her lips. A three-hundred-plus guest list shrunk to a half-hearted twenty-five, so-called friends having fallen away like rats deserting a sinking ship, some exhibiting shocking cruelty on their way out that still hurt to this day.

Violet had endured the occasion only because her mother had insisted on marking the day, spending money they hadn't had for a birthday party no one had wanted to attend, wearing a dress she suspected had come from a charity shop, not the *haute couture* line her mother had insisted it'd come from.

Whatever the genesis of the dress, Violet couldn't fault

its simple but tasteful lines. The dove-grey pleated bodice swept from a shallow V over her cleavage to wrap around her upper arms and back, leaving her shoulders and lower back bare, before the soft chiffon gently moulded her hips and fell away to her ankles.

Since she'd already showered in anticipation of slipping into her pyjamas for an early night, her only task was to slip on the dress, brush and sweep her hair into a tidy chignon, add a simple string of pearls inherited from her grandmother, shoes and make-up, and spritz on her favourite perfume.

Her doorbell went for the second time within half an hour as she was tossing her keys into her small, matching clutch. Her heart attempted to jump into her throat, until she assured herself that royalty didn't conduct such mundane tasks as climbing four flights of dark, dank stairs to knock on the front doors of apartments in buildings within a short sprint of a housing project.

She went to the door, opened it and froze, her jaw sagging at the sight of the man framed in her doorway.

'Do you normally throw open your door with very little regard for your safety?' Prince Zakary Montegova asked coldly.

Violet stared, convinced that the combination of memories, exhaustion and his earlier phone call had colluded into make her hallucinate him. But, no, that steady breathing, those much too incisive grey eyes, that towering, mouthwatering body and especially *that* aftershave convinced her he was all too real.

'I… What are you doing here?'

One sleek, winged eyebrow rose, sarcasm dripping from that small motion.

'I meant you didn't have to come up and get me yourself. You could've called. Or sent one of your bodyguards.' She managed to drag her gaze from him long enough to confirm the security guards without whom he never travelled were indeed present, watchful and crowding her poorly lit hallway.

'And missed this scintillating peek into your life? One that makes me question why you have a peephole and an adequate-looking security chain on your door but chose to use neither?'

That tight bite of irritation had thickened, even as his gaze swept over her from hair to heels, dragging awareness over every inch of skin he scrutinised, all the parts he couldn't see.

It was that bite, that suppressed energy that intensified her awareness, dragged even more unnervingly arresting pieces of Zak Montegova into focus.

The sharp classiness of his bespoke tux highlighting his brooding sexiness.

An innate sensuality overlying a raw masculinity that'd earned him Most Eligible Royal status for more years than Violet cared to count.

'You told me you'd be here in fifteen minutes about… fourteen minutes ago. It doesn't take a wild leap to conclude who was knocking on my door. And, really, are we going to waste more time debating safety protocols? Because I assure you that would take up even more of my precious time.'

'*Your* precious time? You signed a piece of paper, I believe, stating that every moment of your secondment was mine. Have you forgotten?' he drawled, his gaze flickering past her shoulders and into the apartment. Sharp eyes lanced over cheap furniture, cheaper blinds and the stack of conservation books on her coffee table before returning to hers, a little less cynical and a lot more…turbulent. 'Did I interrupt something? Were you entertaining, perhaps?'

Violet pulled the door closer, unwilling to let him see the small sanctuary she'd created for herself. While she kept her space neat and tidy and as homely as a temporary living space could be, the truth was she had very little spare funds to make it any more than functional.

To a man whose kingdom delivered precious gems by the quarry-full, amongst other priceless resources, an apartment like hers would probably make him shudder. But more than that, Violet wanted nothing to escalate his belief that her mother's agenda to marry her off advantageously was hers as well. That she was here in New York for any reason other than to gain as much work experience as she could.

'I think you're a little misguided. You're my mentor for the hours I spend at the trust and perhaps a few extra-curricular duties, but I don't account to you for every moment of my time, and what I do with my private time is none of your business.'

'Are you sure about that?' he asked.

For some reason, her belly somersaulted, and her breath hitched. 'What's that supposed to mean?'

For the longest minute he simply stared at her, eyes slowly narrowing. Then he sharply veered from her doorway, granting her the freedom to shut it behind her.

'You're right. The matter of your security and extra-curricular activities can await another time. I don't wish to keep my minister waiting.'

The fact that he'd simply evaded answering her question puzzled her before she assured herself she didn't really want to know what he'd meant. After all, it had nothing to do with her work.

She told herself that with every step down the long flights of stairs. With every arrogant step that testified that the man who walked beside her was no ordinary man. That he was high born and could trace his ancestry back almost half a millennium.

He gestured her forward at the front door. She stepped through, then startled at his sharp exhalation. A furtive glance over her shoulder showed the briefest flare in the straight blade of his nose. The tiniest hungry flicker in his eyes as they dropped down to her bare back.

A second later he was back under control, prompting her to wonder if she'd imagined that reaction.

Because Zak Montegova didn't betray superfluous emotion. In all things he held himself under supreme control. As if he were still in the military position he'd held in the Montegovan air force in his twenties.

But he had that night.

That hard-packed body had been *alive* with passion, impatiently aroused and breathlessly all-consuming with it. Even though he'd snapped into chilling rebuttal afterwards, she'd experienced that blistering moment when his guard had dropped. When he'd given her a glimpse beneath his armour-plated façade.

For years Violet hadn't quite been able to dismiss that fraction of a moment from her thoughts. Not as easily as the Prince had dismissed her, anyway. Even when she'd imagined she'd seen a residual memory lurking in his eyes the handful of times fate, or her mother, had thrown them together.

But it wasn't until her arrival in New York that she'd known she was mistaken. It'd all been in her imagination. And she needed to kill those thoughts once and for all if she hoped to get ahead in life.

And she had.

For the most part…

But that vital final step eluded her. The last memory of sizzling heat, masterful hands on her body that had ruined her for much longer than she cared to admit. It was why she'd rebuffed any advances from the opposite sex. Because after a few tentative tries she'd known she was wasting time better spent pursuing a fulfilling career. Because even if those advances hadn't eventually been ruined by her mother's meddling or male interest only piqued by the whiff of scandal that followed her name, the memory of Zakary Montegova had always been there, a formidable apparition, rendering every man who came close an unworthy imitation of the accomplished Prince.

The man lauded as a genius. While his brother had been tasked with preserving Montegovan interests, Zak had been tasked with interests abroad. Within a handful of years he'd had heads of states at his beck and call. And that acclaim had gained power and glory with each passing year.

The sights and sounds of New York blasted in the moment they stepped out of her apartment building.

And into the path of a bicycle courier. The cyclist swerved, just as Violet took a hurried step back. Into the hard, towering body of Zak Montegova.

Strong arms gripped her arms to steady her. Fierce eyes drilled into her with a mixture of concern and brusque irritation and that enigmatic gleam that immediately drove the breath from her lungs. Everything fell away.

The courier's irritated shout despite his blatant contravention of cycling laws.

The blare of taxi horns and loud hiss of bus brakes.

The scent of stale hot dogs and hot pretzels.

Only the searing awareness of skin-on-skin contact remained, taking up ever-expanding room in her consciousness until it was the only thing that mattered. Until even breathing became redundant. Secondary to the rush of having her every fear confirmed.

That, regardless of her mother's machinations and Zak's blatant reservations about her presence in New York, she harboured terrible secrets of her own. Secrets she'd taken turns scoffing at and then fearing.

On a sordid little street corner in New York City, Violet accepted the truth that the fairy tale was very much alive.

That the man who'd taken her in his arms, kissed her with soul-stirring expertise while murmuring husky Montegovan words to her, was still very much present beneath that stoic facade. That the man who'd come within a heartbeat of taking her virginity on the night of her eighteenth birthday was still the man she secretly yearned for.

That Zakary Montegova was the reason Violet was, at the ripe old age of twenty-four, still a virgin.

Hard on the heels of the bracing indictment came the realisation that he *knew*. It was there in the blaze of his grey eyes, in the awareness that rippled through his body. In the thumbs brushing her bare skin...testing her weaknesses?

A shiver ran through her body, spreading goosebumps all over her skin.

His gaze released hers for a moment to track her reaction while his hypnotic caress continued. When her nipples began to pearl, he didn't miss it. Didn't miss the acceleration of her heartbeat or the erratic cadence of her breathing.

As if from a distance, she watched his expression change, morph into calculation. It didn't take a genius to guess he was cataloguing his every effect on her for possible use against her.

He made a sound under his breath, a curious cross between a growl and a visceral sound of satisfaction. Of a hunter having stalked his prey into a tight corner.

It was enough to drag Violet out of her stupor. Enough to stress the urgent need to redouble her efforts to resist her mother's intentions.

But most of all to prevent Zak from confirming the truth.

At all costs.

CHAPTER TWO

WEAK MOMENTS HAD the power to bring down kingdoms.

Zakary Montegova knew this all too well.

So when Violet scurried away from him towards the limo idling at the kerb as if he'd suddenly contracted a flesh-eating plague, he let her go, following at a slower pace and absolutely rejecting what the sight of her smooth bare back and pert, rounded bottom did to his libido.

Dio mio, hadn't his father delivered an abject lesson in weakness from beyond the grave? The repercussions of it had been deep and traumatic, and still haunted the royal Montegovan household to this day in the form of his much more reserved and circumspect brother, Remi. In the form of his mother's quiet anguish, well hidden behind the façade of royal duty and the solemn, defiant refusal to be cowed by any circumstance. It was well documented in the antics of his illegitimate half-brother, Jules, the physical manifestation of their father's weakness.

Most of all, it was what he'd witnessed within hours of his father's death and the revelation of the late King's infidelity. How close the seat of power had come to being usurped by greedy generals and shameless opportunists, eager to capitalise on the kingdom's instability; that had shown Zak just how precarious temptation could be.

Weak moments had the power to bring *him* down.

It was why he led a life of hard work, harder diligence and zero trust in his fellow man. Why no woman had even the smallest chance of claiming him. Why he was more than content to leave the production of heirs to his brother, the Crown Prince.

So why had he allowed Violet Barringhall to burrow beneath his skin six years ago?

He'd nearly refused his mother's request to attend her birthday party. He'd had better things to do than indulge his mother's misguided friendship with the notorious Margot Barringhall, the infamous gossipmonger, opportunist and tabloid lover.

Everything he stood against. But his mother had insisted.

And from the first moment he'd seen the grown-up version of the girl he'd met very briefly only twice before, Zak had been unable to take his eyes off Violet. The hour he'd intended to spend at her party had turned to two, then four. Despite his distaste at the increasingly drunken behaviour of her so-called friends, he'd lingered. Followed her out into her mother's garden, enticed by the timid but alluring feminine wiles she'd seemed determined to flex.

At some point he'd believed he was testing himself, seeing how far her enthralment would last. A misguided attempt at immersion therapy, over-exposure to several hours' worth of temptation after which he'd walk away, triumphant over the pressure in his groin and the bewildering need to touch her. Taste her.

Find a mundane answer to why Lady Violet Barringhall intrigued him.

So he'd followed. He'd touched. He'd *tasted*. And craved more with an unending hunger that had dogged his waking hours for months. Driven him to investigate the Barringhalls. He'd felt no guilt over it, as it was in fact a practice he'd followed since his father's death. He'd thoroughly vetted every affiliation to his family, tenuous or otherwise, ensuring the events following his father's death never occurred again.

But he'd also secretly entertained the possibility of a liaison with Violet down the line.

Only he'd discovered there was nothing remotely honourable about the Barringhalls.

They were in hock up to their eyeballs, the Earl having depleted his substantial family resources through a dizzying series of bad investments and gluttony before his untimely death. After which his wife, Countess Margot Barringhall, had taken up the mantle, frantic to safeguard her way of life by indiscriminate dalliance with the press and, when they had come of age, attempting to marry off her daughters to any half-decent man with a large bank balance who was thirsty for a shoddy little title.

Zak's disappointment in the discovery had been searing and shocking, his fury at nearly falling into Margot Barringhall's well-laid trap elevating her and her daughters to the top of his to-be-watched list.

The phone call from his mother three months ago with the secondment request had fortified Zak's guard.

Since her arrival, he'd thrown every menial task at her to push her into admitting defeat and pleading for her mother to intercede on her behalf.

The crunch point had never arrived. Perversely, he'd detested being proven wrong about her, and had piled more work onto her slim shoulders. She'd raised her game higher, exhibiting a finely tuned talent for understanding the needs of his trust, especially the work he undertook for the less privileged.

But Zak was rarely impressed. Violet Barringhall was a tougher cookie than he'd given her credit for, but the reminder of her body straining against his, her shockingly sexy little whimpers and greedy hands, were testament to her hidden skills. And that sometimes shy demeanour that hid a tart tongue? *Si*, it'd come within a whisker of rousing his jaded humour.

And therein lay the pitfalls. Allowing himself to be impressed, *tempted*, by her had nearly resulted in a gross error of judgement that could've cost his family untold misery.

It was why he stayed away from tall, statuesque women with silky, chestnut hair and eyes the colour of the turquoise-blue waters that sparkled beneath the Montegovan sun.

He slid into the car, watched her cross her legs in a curiously elegant way that effectively angled her body away from his. Poise, no doubt drilled into her in that expensive finishing school her family had ill-afforded, was evident in her ramrod-straight spine, the hands folded neatly over her clutch in her lap, and perfectly angled jaw.

The only thing giving all that *decorum* away was the pulse leaping at her throat. Her very silky, very smooth and supple throat. Creamy skin he wanted to stroke. To taste.

Basta!

He stirred in his seat, registered what he was doing and froze.

Dio mio, since when did he *fidget*?

He told himself it was his annoyance that made him glance over her body, over her shadowed cleavage that gave a tantalising peek of her breasts. It was annoyance causing the fever in his veins.

'You're meant to be taking notes, yet you don't seem to have brought any note-taking equipment with you.'

Shrewd blue eyes met his and...*mocked* him? 'Perhaps because it's no longer necessary to bring a whole stationery cupboard to take notes. I have an app on my phone—approved by the trust, I believe—to take notes and transcribe digitally. Depending on how quickly you want it, I can have it ready in an hour.'

'And if I want it sooner?' he asked, simply because his mood was decidedly testy and she was the cause of it.

'Then I'd have to wonder why you're even bothering to

attend the fundraiser if you have far more pressing matters to deal with. Don't get me wrong, I know you're a master at multi-tasking but it would help to know what I'm supposed to prioritise.'

Their arrival at his embassy put paid to his errant thoughts and, thankfully, the need to dissect thereal cause of his disgruntlement. 'Let's go and find out, shall we?'

He stepped out, ingrained courtesy dictating he hold out his hand to her.

She accepted his assistance, slid out gracefully but almost immediately attempted to regain her hand. Zak released her but not before he once again registered the smooth, supple warmth of her skin. The need to keep touching her.

General Pierre Alvardo, Montegova's defence minister, approached the moment they were inside the vast hallway of the Montegovan embassy.

'Your Highness, thank you for meeting me. This matter is urgent or I wouldn't have interrupted your evening.'

'I'll be the judge of that.' Zak had accepted the meeting because Alvardo tended to be a little trigger happy. His mother had her hands full with parliamentary duties and his brother, Crown Prince Remi, was on a diplomatic mission in the Middle East.

Alvardo slid a glance at Violet, then addressed his next request in Montegovan.

Zak stopped him with a halting hand. 'You may address me in English, Alvardo. Lady Barringhall has signed a confidentiality contract and knows the consequences of breaking it.'

Beside him, Violet gave a sanguine smile that somehow tunnelled straight into his bloodstream, heating it up several more degrees. 'Lady Barringhall hasn't forgotten, Your Highness. She doesn't need to be reminded.'

Alvardo's eyes widened but he hadn't risen to defence minister without learning a thing or two about diplomacy.

In the conference room, Zak waited for Violet to be seated before taking his place at the head of the table. The moment she set her phone to record, he got straight to the point.

'Is this about the group of dissidents you alerted us to two months ago?'

Alvardo nodded. 'Intelligence reports they've doubled in number and may be planning an insurgency in Playagova in the near future.'

Zak tensed. 'May be? You're not completely certain of their plans?'

Alvardo's gaze grew cagey. 'We haven't been able to infiltrate the group as easily as we'd hoped.'

Zak's eyes narrowed. 'You're here to seek leave to openly pursue them?' he surmised.

His minister nodded. 'As the Queen's appointed head of the Montegovan military, you will have to give express instructions for an active investigation into the group.'

'Even though such an act could fuel anxiety, cause undue panic?' he countered.

'I believe it's a small price to pay for absolute certainty.'

'I don't.'

Zak felt Violet's gaze on him. He glanced at her, registered the relief in her eyes before she broke eye contact to fiddle needlessly with her phone.

'But… Your Highness.' Alvardo paused, and Zak got the notion he was measuring his words. 'I'm of the opinion that this could get out of hand very quickly if not immediately dealt with.'

'Then redouble your efforts to turn *may be* into concrete evidence. The Montegovan people have been through enough without causing ripples with unfounded rumours. Maintain surveillance without engaging and report back to me when something changes.' Until then he'd make his own investigations, double check the general's report.

With his mother's recent but as yet unannounced intention to step down from the throne in favour of Remi, the situation would need extremely careful monitoring. The last thing Montegova needed with its recent history was another shaky period. 'That will be all.'

The general rose, gave a grave bow and left the room.

Zak noted Violet's heavy silence as he escorted her back out to the car.

It wasn't until they cleared Midtown traffic and were heading towards the Upper East Side, where the fundraiser was being held, that he turned to her.

'Ask your questions. I can see you're about to burst from the effort of maintaining your silence.'

She pressed plump lips together for a short moment. 'Is there really a threat to your country?'

He shrugged. 'There's always a threat. The trick is to separate the salient from the white noise, as it were.'

'But what the general said…it all sounded urgent.'

'Alvardo is a defence minister. He believes he wouldn't be doing his job if he didn't advocate fire and brimstone at every turn.'

She frowned. 'Are you sure? It seems a little more than that.'

'Probably because it is,' Zak confirmed, then wondered why he was giving her this leeway, letting her into secrets that might come back to bite him.

'And you're happy to go along with such dire predictions? Are you really okay with such blatant…warmongering?'

'I've learned to look beneath the surface, always. He makes his reports. I investigate further where I need to. The truth of the situation always comes out in the end.' He couldn't stem bitterness that stemmed directly from the secret his father had kept for over twenty years, only to have it explode in their faces even before the dirt had settled over his final resting place. But his statement was also aimed at Violet, more specifically at the plans she'd concocted with her mother.

He glanced at her, noted how her lashes swept down and away, pretending interest in the passing scenery outside the window. *Si*, Lady Violet Barringhall, like her mother, clearly thought they were pulling the wool over his eyes with this stint at his trust.

'And do you think this situation requires serious investigation? Are people really plotting to bring the kingdom down?' she asked after a moment with wide-eyed interest that appeared genuine. But then her interest would be genuine, wouldn't it, if she had aspirations of elevating herself from Lady to Princess?

Zak shrugged with an ease he didn't feel deep down. 'There are those who believe the era of the monarchy is long past. That the people should dispense with the royal house altogether.' He gauged her reaction. While her expression looked a little troubled, there wasn't the cutting desperation he'd expected at the possibility of her coveted position evaporating before her eyes.

Perhaps she was a better actress than he'd initially credited her with being.

'And what do you say to that?'

Centuries-old pride and the warrior's clamour of his forebears drew only one answer from him. 'My ancestors didn't carve out a kingdom through blood and battle only to hand it over to a disgruntled few who believe they know what's right for my people. Montegova isn't ruled by a power-hungry figurehead who merely sits on the throne and collects taxes at the end of a fiscal year. My mother and brother are both active members of parliament. Their votes are just two among many that operate under a system of check and balances agreed by law. As the current head of the monarchy, the Queen has certain rights, granted, but she's not above the law. Whatever injustices are felt should be addressed through the legal system, not through uprisings.'

'That's easy to say, though, some would say. Didn't your ancestors stamp out dissension when there were bloody revolutions?'

He allowed himself a smile that didn't quite unfreeze the chill in his chest, not when the memory of how close to chaos Montegova had come a mere decade ago echoed through him. 'Precisely. So why follow the same tired route when we can forge new ones? Innovate, don't imitate, isn't that the saying?'

'Why are you pretending to be flippant about this?' she asked.

Zak tensed, despising the extra layer of disgruntlement her incisive observation triggered. 'Perhaps I'm wondering what your motives are. Your task was simply to take notes. Why the sudden interest in Montegova?' he tossed back at her.

She floundered momentarily before her composure snapped back into place. 'I work for you, for the time being. Is it really so strange for me to take an interest, considering I have an affiliation with Montegova? Or have you forgotten that my mother is half-Montegovan?'

He hadn't forgotten, neither had he missed how effectively the Barringhalls used that fact when it suited them financially. 'And how many times have you visited the homeland you have a *quarter* claim to?'

She flushed, even though her gaze stayed defiantly on his. 'Not as often as I would've liked—'

'By that you mean never, am I right?'

'We both know I've never visited Montegova.'

Perhaps it was time to root her out, turn the tables on this scheme by the Barringhalls and be done with this woman who tempted him like no other.

'According to your résumé, you've been to the other side of the world. The life you choose to live on social media is fond of screaming that fact but you've never bothered to visit the homeland of your non-British ancestors on the other side of Europe? I'm sure you'll excuse me if I find your concern for the state of affairs in my kingdom some-what...lacking.'

'My travels were funded by charitable donations pains-takingly gathered over four years because I was determined to make a difference. And if by life on social media, you mean my *job*, then yes. It's called raising awareness.'

His lips twisted. 'There is a fine line between raising awareness and raising one's own profile.'

'Is there? How would you know? Isn't your royal web-page managed by a team of social media experts? Or are you one of those royals who can't resist having a secret profile so you can play the voyeur on other people's lives?'

He allowed himself a riling smile. 'If I do possess such a page, rest assured, I won't divulge it to you.'

Hot emotion flashed through her eyes. But again it was swiftly swept under the cloak of utter composure. And why did that normally laudable ability suddenly grate on his nerves?

'Because you, like everyone else, believe every single thing you hear about my family?' she demanded, her tone holding a chilled note of censure. As if she was the one dis-appointed in him, not the other way around.

'The evidence is hard to refute but I invite you to try.'

Her lips pursed again and, like a fool, he latched onto the motion, recalling far too vividly the taste and supple-ness of her lower lip. The eagerness of her response. Did she still make those insane little sounds when aroused?

'No, thank you. Far be it from me to waste my time on

a futile task. Besides, we've arrived,' she announced with more than a little relief in her voice.

Zak flicked a glance out his window, his ire increasing. He'd been so absorbed in her he'd lost all sense of time and place. He ignored his driver's presence beside the back door and concentrated on Violet. On the answer she'd given him. Had she truly just refused a silver-plated invitation to interact with him?

Zak could honestly say he didn't recall the last time the words *no, thanks* had fallen from a woman's lips in his company.

And again he was…intrigued. He stared into the blue eyes regarding him with a touch of wariness and…reproof.

'Your Highness—'

'Zak.'

Her eyes widened. 'What?'

'You may call me Zak when we're not in a formal or professional setting. I'll leave it to your discretion,' he said, reeling a little from the words falling from his own mouth.

She didn't speak the words but the refrain of *no, thanks*, blazed in her eyes.

Another first.

'We're going to be late, Your Highness.' She aimed a pointed gaze at the door. 'And I don't wish be blamed for your tardiness.'

A peculiar little blaze fired through him, fanning higher the longer he looked into her eyes. He was a prince. Second in line to the throne of a small but infinitely mighty kingdom. Not very many people dared to defy him.

Violet Barringhall was exhibiting definite signs of defiance.

The urge to put her in her place resurged. But it had a different slant to it this time. There were so many ways to deliver one's point. To those who sought to seed mistrust and dissent in his kingdom. To those who sought to gain financially on the back of his family name.

Why not try a different solution to this problem? Take that immersive therapy he'd mocked to another level. Send the Barringhalls a message once and for all.

She blinked, drawing his attention to her wide, alluring eyes. The flawless skin of her throat and neck. Lust kicked hard in his groin, reminding him that he hadn't indulged himself in a while.

She'd flashed those eyes at him just like that on her birthday. Well, two could play at this game the Barringhalls had started.

Si, it really was the perfect solution.

Decided, he flicked his wrist and his driver eased the door open.

Zak stepped out to a frenzy of paparazzi flashbulbs. Ignoring them, he offered his hand to Violet, this time holding onto her as she stepped out onto the red carpet.

In her heels, she came up to his shoulder, the perfect angle for him to gaze down at for a beat before the inevitable personal questions were shouted at him.

He didn't answer, of course. Pandering to the media was beneath him, and he'd learned long ago that the tabloid press printed what they wanted regardless of his answers or, indeed, the truth.

But when they caught sight of Violet and tripled their questions, he allowed an enigmatic smile to play on his lips as he tucked her arm into his and escorted her inside.

The paradigm had shifted.

Violet couldn't pinpoint exactly what had happened or when. But as she walked beside Zak though the throng of designer-clad guests, she sensed an edgier purpose from him. Instinctively, she knew it wasn't the challenge of attempting to meet his impossibly high standards.

Whatever Zak had up his sleeve was *personal*. Aimed at her.

It lurked in the shrewd, too-long gazes that repeatedly slanted her way as he guided her around the opulent ballroom. Halfway through the first circuit, she knew she needed to extricate herself from him.

His tight schedule, even at social functions, provided the perfect excuse. 'You have three pre-dinner drinks. The first is with the Bolivian attaché. Here he comes now,' she said briskly, hoping that flinging them both into business mode would throw him off whatever scent he seemed determined to hunt down.

Zak nodded without taking his eyes off the person he was saying goodbye to, then skilfully intercepted her with a hand on her elbow before she could walk away. 'Stay. Your presence will curtail his tendency to drone on ad nauseam. You might also pick up a tip or two to take back to your institution when you leave in a few months.'

The reminder that this position was temporary shouldn't have annoyed her, considering she'd been praying for it to end a short while ago. Perhaps it abraded her nerves because he stated it with that narrow-eyed, watchful suspicion? 'I'll stay if you think I'll be useful. My role is to assist, after all.'

'Do I detect a little displeasure in your tone, Lady Barringhall?'

Violet.

She barely stopped herself from issuing the invitation. She wouldn't. He could use that mocking tone all he liked. Right up until she extricated herself permanently from him.

'Of course not,' she said with a smile manufactured straight from the depths of the decorum rulebook.

She ignored his droll expression as he greeted the attaché, sending him on his way the moment the man's conversation grew circuitous. But after he'd introduced her to the next person with that faintly mocking tone once more, she'd had enough. 'Why do you keep throwing my title in people's faces?'

'I don't know what you mean.'

Ignoring the blatantly false claim of obliviousness, she pressed on. 'You've been in a…mood since we arrived. Is this some sort of test?'

'Everything is a test, Lady Barringhall. If you don't know that by now, then I've been wasting my time.'

'I don't mean professionally and you know it. This feels personal. Did I do something to offend you?'

The only hint that she may have strayed near a bullseye with her question was in the brief flaring of his nostrils. Then he was back under supreme control. 'I merely introduced you with your correct title. I fail to see why you would feel attacked by it.'

To push the issue felt like overkill. And yet… 'Perhaps we should clear the air. Lay things out in the open?'

His eyes gleamed. 'Ah, now we get to the heart of the matter. Is this where you confess?'

She frowned. 'Excuse me? Confess what?'

'That this so-called role of yours is just hiding your true purpose here,' he said, an edge in his tone.

'And what's my true purpose, pray tell? No, wait, let me guess. You think it's some sort of ploy to land myself somewhere in your private life? Or, goodness, perhaps even in your bed?'

That earned her more emotion. His eyes blazed wildly and ferociously, just like they had that night, before he ruthlessly smothered it. But it didn't die completely. She felt its latent heat as his gaze drilled into her. 'Is your ultimate goal to land in my *bed*? You should've said this straight out, Violet. Then we could've dispensed with all this…pretence.'

Fire intensified, flaring out from her pelvis to engulf her whole body. 'You're deliberately twisting my words. I don't want to end up in your bed. Hell, I don't want to go anywhere near your bedroom!'

A few heads turned, and she flushed as eyebrows went up at her hot, charged denial.

Just then a discreet little chime announced the end of the champagne reception. Violet breathed in relief.

'Saved by the bell but definitely to be continued, I think,' he rasped as they drifted towards an even more opulently decorated ballroom where the main event was being held.

'No, it won't,' she whispered fiercely. 'I hate to disappoint you but I've said all I'm going to say on the matter. I don't care what you think my motives are, but I'd thank you to—'

'You don't care? Have you forgotten that one major reason you're here is to get your hands on my invaluable letter of recommendation?'

'Are you threatening to withhold it unless I indulge you in your silly little game? Is that what this is about?'

His mouth twisted. 'Let's not throw around accusations on who is playing games with whom, Lady Barringhall.' His voice was silky, like a stiletto knife sliding through butter. All without losing an ounce of his arrogant composure. Hell, he even nodded greetings to a few guests in the process of cutting her down.

She refused to be cowed. 'You didn't answer my question. I've done everything you've asked of me since I arrived in New York. But if I'm wasting my time, at least have the balls to tell me so we can be rid of each other sooner rather than later,' she dared, her heart banging hard against her ribcage. She didn't want to risk irritating him more than she already seemed to be doing, but she didn't want to throw away all her efforts either.

They reached their designated high table and he slid back her chair, his strong, elegant hands braced on the sides as he waited for her to be seated.

Violet moved, incredibly aware of his proximity, of his scent and the powerful body barely leashed beneath the trappings of civilised clothing. Aware of his complete focus on her. She called on every crumb of composure she possessed, thankful when she took her seat without stumbling.

But then he lowered his head to align with hers, drawing a wild shiver as he murmured for her ears alone, 'A few weeks of running around in my office, dispensing effortless English charm, isn't going to quite cut it. If you want to earn my regard, you'll need to do a lot more than lackey work. And as for my balls, Lady Barringhall, I'd caution you not to involve them in our conversations. At least, not in this setting. Later, though…who knows? I just might accommodate you.'

Heat flared into her cheeks, whipping up a wild tornado that centred between her thighs. She refused to be thrown by the images he evoked. Nevertheless, it took considerable scrambling to get her brain to formulate an answer. 'What do I need to do to prove my worth?' she demanded once he was seated, frustration building in her chest.

'You want to prove your worth? The trust is in the process of building eco-lodges in Tanzania. It's a tourism initiative in partnership with the government to provide long-term income to the area. Tell me what you would bring to the table in this project.'

Violet ruthlessly curbed her excitement. With a few words, he'd described everything she hoped to aspire to in her career. But she didn't put it past him to dangle an offer in her face only to snatch it up the moment she expressed an interest. That gleam in his eyes had only intensified in the last few minutes, his focus on her almost rabid in its fervour.

'How many lodges?'

'Thirty to start off with catering to the discerning and

environmentally-conscious tourist in mind. Twice that in phases two and three.'

'When are you looking to vet volunteers? I could help you with that. Weed out those wanting a free ride against those committed to truly making a difference.'

'There are a few on the ground already but the majority are lined up to be vetted in the next week or two.'

She shook her head. 'The rainy season starts in less than three months. If you don't want the project severely disrupted, you need to move quicker than that.'

A smile ghosted over his lips and Violet suspected he'd been testing her.

Her shoulders went back. She lifted her chin and stared him straight in the eyes. 'You want to test my true commitment? Include me in the project. My secondment is up in about the time it'll take for this first phase to be done. Let me prove to you that this isn't just some flight of fancy.'

He wasn't impressed by her declaration. If anything, his scepticism increased. 'You wouldn't be the first royal seeking to elevate their status by affiliating themselves with a project like this. Just so we're clear, that's not going to happen here.'

'All I'm asking is that you suspend your suspicion of my motives for a few weeks and let me do what I came here to do. Or are you so cynical that you won't even give me that chance?'

His smile turned hard, edgy. 'You seem in a mood to throw around taunts.'

'I'm defending my character. I'm a hard worker. Take my word for it or let my actions speak for themselves.'

Stormcloud eyes pinned her to her seat. But before he could respond, a hush descended, drawing their attention to the podium as the patron of the fundraising charity rose to make her welcoming speech. The world-renowned socialite, known for her skills in raising millions for charitable causes, repeatedly glanced over at Zak as she spoke.

Despite being over a decade older than him, her interest was blatant, a fact, Violet suspected, that had contributed to her hosting this event.

For a cynical moment Violet wondered if Zak had taken advantage of it. Whether he'd had even a moment's pause before aligning himself with a woman whose gaze caressed his face even as she delivered a charming, quick-witted speech.

She only registered that she'd been staring at him for an indecent amount of time when his gaze swung sharply to her, one eyebrow cocked at whatever he read in her expression.

She resisted the urge to drop her gaze, allowed hers to linger before, feigning boredom, she turned towards the podium as the socialite ended her speech to applause.

Violet couldn't fault her. As her own mother had repeatedly striven to maximise every opportunity by hosting such events, people were more prone to opening their wallets when in a good mood.

And the sight of Prince Zak Montegova, rising with masterful grace and long-limbed elegance to step up to the podium, made them feel extra-special.

His speech was a sublime combination of wit, gravitas and arrogant challenge, rousing consciences and stirring sluggish apathy. Heads nodded and any remaining sceptics couldn't help but be moved by the video presentation of the trust's needs, especially in deprived communities.

'And just so you'll appreciate the urgency of my latest project, I've been informed by Lady Violet Barringhall, my newly appointed special advisor on our latest project in Tanzania, that time is even more of the essence if we're to meet our goals. Which means you'll also need to move fast or this particular train will leave without you. And if you miss this one, you won't be guaranteed a seat on the next one.'

And, simply because everyone in the room wanted a connection with the Royal House of Montegova and its representative Prince, they laughed a little more eagerly, their glances sharper as they turned to her, prying and assessing whether *she* was the conduit to their ultimate prize—access to Zak Montegova.

But Violet wasn't interested in them. She was wholly consumed by Zak's revelation. Her heart banged anew when he stared at her in blatant challenge for a sizzling few seconds, absorbed the applause at the end of his speech, before stepping off the podium.

He neither paused nor smiled in acknowledgement of the accolades dropped in his wake as he returned to the table.

Soft music struck up from a string quartet as he resumed his seat.

'You couldn't have told me before you made the announcement?' she asked, wondering why her excitement, while effervescent—because this was what she'd dreamed of for as long as she could recall—was tinged with an even sharper thrill she suspected had nothing to do with her new role and everything to do with the man who'd granted it.

'I believe this is the moment in the process where you thank me for giving you this opportunity?' he drawled silkily, dark grey eyes fixed on her face.

Violet swallowed her sharp reply. Regardless of how the package had been delivered it was the content, the chance to start to make a difference, that mattered. 'Thank you for the opportunity. And before you taunt me by asking me if I'm up to the task, I assure you I am.'

'You urged me to test your mettle. Consider this the first lesson. But I'll be watching you every step of the way. One misstep and you're done.'

'There won't be any,' she stressed, for him and especially

for herself. She couldn't afford any, not if she wanted to drag herself out of the shadow of her parents' misdeeds.

'Good. We leave in seven days. You can have tomorrow morning off to pack.'

Something wild and urgent fluttered in her belly. *'We?'*

'Did I not mention it? I'll be in on the ground in Tanzania too. Which means you'll be working directly under me,' he said, his voice deep, weighted with evocative meaning that sent blood surging through her body to concentrate traitorously between her thighs.

He stared at her long enough to register the effect of his words on her. Then he turned away and addressed the other guests at the table.

Violet sat back, attempted to absorb the swift turn of events, and the image she couldn't erase from her mind— of her trapped beneath the sensual power and might of Zak Montegova—quickly enough.

The gauntlet had been thrown down, and her with it, right into the spotlight. Perhaps in more ways than one.

Either way, it was up to her to show him, to show everyone, that she wasn't just a tainted title, biding her time until a rich, preferably titled man swept her off her feet and answered all her mother's prayers.

CHAPTER THREE

TANZANIA WAS HOT, humid and stunningly beautiful. Even the humid bustle of Dar es Salaam held a unique vibe that escalated Violet's excitement as they disembarked from Zak's private jet and headed out of Tanzania's largest city.

Air-conditioned SUVs allayed a little of the discomfort travelling into the heart of the country caused with pot-holed roads, but Violet absorbed every second of it, still pinching herself that she'd managed to get herself into the field so quickly.

Their final destination, Lake Ngoro, was still a good two hours away, according to the satnav, when they stopped for lunch.

Despite the stunning and picturesque vista, the restaurant was little more than a few thatched huts with tables and chairs grouped under shaded umbrellas. When the procession of four SUVs stopped, Violet hid a grimace as the suited bodyguards alighted stiffly and formed a loose semi-circle around their Prince.

'Something annoying you already?' Zak enquired, his laconic drawl suggesting he wasn't surprised. 'The heat perhaps? Or the sparse surroundings? Five-star establishments a little thin on the ground for you?'

Violet ground her teeth and breathed through her irritation as a waiter hurried towards them. 'None of the above. If you must know, I was thinking that six bodyguards seem a little...excessive, don't you think?'

'Protocol dictates it needs to be this way. And I'd rather

not incur my mother's wrath by going against her wishes,' he added with a wry twist of his lips.

Queen Isadora was a formidable woman. Even though she and her mother were friends, Violet had met the Queen only twice in her life. Both times she'd been awed by the woman's utter poise and the shrewd intelligence that shone from grey eyes she'd passed to her sons, along with her strength and resilience.

'Does their presence ever get overwhelming?'

He cracked open a bottle of iced water and poured her a glass before filling his own. 'That's like asking if breathing is tedious. It is what it is.'

Her fingers curled around the chilled glass. 'Would you change it if you could?'

Despite the shades concealing his eyes, she felt his probing gaze. 'Why would I want to change a status only a fraction of people ever get to experience? I'm deemed one of the luckiest men in the world to be surrounded by yes men and women all too eager to obey my every command,' he stated with a thick layer of cynicism.

'And yet your tone suggests otherwise,' she replied.

For a fraction of a moment he seemed startled by the observation. As if he'd let something slip he hadn't intended to. Then his face resumed its stoic mask. 'I was taught not only to appreciate the advantages of my status but also to help preserve it. And to deal effectively with those parasites who would attempt to leech their way into riches on my family's coattails.'

It didn't take a genius to know she'd been lumped in with that deplorable crowd. 'But you don't mind using those yes men and women to accomplish your goals?'

His eyes narrowed. 'Are we being specific here, Violet? Are you asking me if I take advantage of my status?'

The man-eating eyes of that fundraising socialite flashed

to mind and she tried to curb the curious sting in her chest. 'Do you?'

'I earn my dues in business. And in pleasure. No one has left my presence dissatisfied. Unless they absolutely deserved it, of course.'

The urge to pluck the sunglasses off his face so she could read his expression warred with the very real need to deny that they were speaking about the same thing—the night of her eighteenth birthday. Had she deserved to be left dissatisfied like that?

And why was he referring to it now?

The waiter's arrival with platters of food put paid to the dangerous train of thought she seemed to stray into with maddening frequency.

'Are you done?' He nodded at her plate twenty minutes later, a frown in his voice.

She looked down at her plate. The food had been tasty so she attributed her elusive appetite to Zak's presence more than anything else. 'Turns out I'm not very hungry.'

His lips firmed but he rose without saying a word.

Back in the SUV, Zak Montegova handled the vehicle with effortless grace, his body packed with latent power that repeatedly drove the very air from her lungs each time she glanced his way. Bouncing over potholes and being jostled about, it was difficult not to be aware of her own body and its close proximity to Zak's.

So she was relieved to arrive two long hours later, to breathe the fresh, clean air of Lake Ngoro, the mostly flat green landscape where Zak had sited the Trust's eco-lodges.

Events had proceeded at breakneck pace after the fundraiser. As she'd predicted, donations had flooded in from the great and good, easily ensuring that they could fund another five projects within the year.

And Zak's confirmation on Monday that the rains were

indeed expected in a few weeks sparked an urgency for the trip. Violet had read through hundreds of résumés, sat in on in-person and video conference interviews, and grilled each volunteer until she was certain the sixty-five they'd chosen would be up to the daunting task of constructing the eco-lodges in time.

As she looked around now, she was gratified to see that the local construction crew who'd already been on site for two weeks were already at the final stages of laying the foundations.

A man broke away from a group of workers hammering a sign board into the ground and hurried towards them. His dark bronze skin, curly mahogany hair and light eyes indicated a mixed heritage. Despite the sweat pouring down his face and sticking to his tie-dyed T-shirt, his grin was infectious and as open as his outstretched hand.

'Hey, there. I'm Peter Awadhi, foreman slash friendly face slash official representative of the Tourist Board. We've spoken a few times on the phone but let me formally welcome you to Tanzania…um… Prince…er… Your Highness.'

Violet hid a smile as he stumbled over Zak's title.

Zak shook his hand. 'Zak is fine,' he offered, although he didn't return the man's smile.

Peter nodded, then glanced at her.

She held out her hand. 'I'm Violet Barringhall. Special advisor, volunteer co-ordinator and general dogsbody.'

'Ah, you're the new one in charge of the volunteers? Sweet. I have a few requests to swing by you later when you've had a chance to settle in.'

'Of course. That's what I'm here for.'

His grin widened and Zak's face soured further. 'Are our tents ready?' Zak asked.

Peter released her hand, looked over towards the SUVs and shouted instructions in Kiswahili at the group erecting the sign. 'They are. I'll have your luggage taken to your assigned tents when you're ready.'

'We will. The sample lodge is ready to view?' Zak asked.

Peter nodded. 'In the west compound, as you instructed.'

'Take me there, I'd like to inspect it.'

'Sure thing,' Peter replied, in no way daunted by Zak's hit-the-ground-running attitude.

'When we're done, I'd like a tour of the rest of the site, if that's not too much trouble?' Violet asked.

Zak frowned. 'We just arrived. You should rest.'

She shook her head. 'I'm not tired and I've been cooped up in the car for hours. I'd like to stretch my legs and familiarise myself with the landscape in preparation for when the volunteers arrive tomorrow.'

His lips firmed and he clicked his fingers. One of his bodyguards rushed forward and a low exchange took place in Montegovan. Before Violet could blink, a wide-brimmed straw hat magically appeared. Zak held it out to her. 'Heatstroke is a serious issue here. I'd hate to have to use the chopper on our very first day.'

She'd packed a hat for herself but with her luggage still stowed in the SUV, she had no choice but to accept Zak's offering.

'Thanks.' She pulled on the hat, glad for the shade it offered.

They made their way from the parking area to the heart of the site, where the large building that would house the reception, restaurant and spa were located.

The construction crew were in the final stages of pouring concrete for the foundations. The handful of volunteers who'd been on site from the beginning would leave as soon as the new volunteers Violet had helped select arrived to start their work erecting the lodges.

They bypassed the central building and she spotted a sleek helicopter, the one Zak had referred to, on the far north side of the flat landscape. Its discreet little red and white cross caught her attention.

'Why the medical chopper? I didn't think it'd be needed at a project like this,' she said to Peter.

He glanced briefly at Zak before he answered. 'This isn't strictly a medical helicopter but it's useful since the nearest medical facility is thirty miles away. It's purely a worst-case scenario option.'

Of course, with the VIP royal who happened to be second in line to the Montegovan throne on site, safeguarding him was paramount. Looking closer, Violet spotted the monogram of the Montegovan royal house on the tail fin of the aircraft, confirming her theory.

Zak sent her a sidelong glance. 'Before you think the pampered Prince has a chopper on tap to deal with his splinters, you should know that the chef in charge of feeding the whole camp happens to be eight months pregnant. She refuses to leave before her rotation is up in two weeks. The helicopter is primarily for her in case she goes into early labour.'

Shame lanced her and she was glad for the wide brim of the hat hiding her chagrin. Zak's mocking gaze returned to the path as they left the first row of lodges and headed west.

The eco-lodge came into view as they rounded an acacia tree.

The single storey building was functional, compact but beautiful, designed for a small family. It blended into the landscape and had a simple wraparound veranda at the front to make the most of west-facing sunlight.

Zak stepped onto the veranda and opened the front door.

The functional theme was echoed inside with an open-plan living room and kitchen, and two small bedrooms tucked into the back of the house. But it was the hidden extras that Violet was interested in.

'Bath water is recycled into sanitary plumbing?' she asked.

Zak nodded. 'And solar panels on the roof at the back provide energy. A central borehole has been dug ready to harvest natural artesian water and rain. There's a large borehole for the whole village.'

According to the report she'd read back in New York, the eco-lodges had been a joint-design between Zak and Tanzanian architects to exact specifications, with as much locally sourced materials as possible, after which they were constructed and flat-packed in Montegova and shipped three weeks ago. It was clear this project was close to his heart as he inspected every corner of the dwelling, pointing out areas he wanted rechecked and improved in the yet-to-be-built units.

Peter answered every query, providing intelligent solutions when Zak demanded them. Before they left the sample house, it was clear why he'd been chosen as foreman.

Thinking she would be left alone with Peter to conduct her tour, she inhaled sharply when Zak fell into step beside her. Violet refused to glance his way, a little resentful that he brimmed with vitality after endless hours in the vehicle, whereas she felt hot and sticky and wilted.

They were circling back to the heart of the site when a volunteer arrived with a query for Peter. He made his excuses and left, leaving her alone with Zak.

'First impressions?' Zak asked.

She was impressed. She couldn't deny it, so she didn't. 'It's exceptional.'

Zak nodded. 'There will also be a Montegovan specialist on site for the first three months to train homeowners on how to fix basic things should they go wrong.'

There was a pulse of pride in his voice that threatened to destabilise the picture she'd drawn of him. Threatened to soften a place inside her she needed to keep under tight guard. Lofty thoughts of the charming Prince saving the less privileged belonged in fairy tales.

'Should I take that frown to mean you don't approve?'

She shook her head. 'I approve of all this. But I'm wondering about you,' she blurted. 'You have thousands at your command to do all of this. Why are you here?'

He'd taken off his shades when they'd entered the lodge and now speared her with the full force of his grey eyes. 'You want to know why I'm supervising a project that bears my name?' he asked, his tone bone-dry.

'Don't you worry that people will wonder what a Harvard-educated Mediterranean prince needs to prove by digging around in the dirt? That this is really some PR stunt? Like you said, it wouldn't be the first time a privileged royal did this sort of thing in the hope of gaining points with the media.'

His shrug was chock-full of dismissive arrogance. 'I'm in the unique position of not having to impress anyone or caring what anyone thinks.'

Because he had the advantage of status, wealth and drop-dead gorgeous good looks?

'Not even that you want to make a difference?' she pressed, a little unsure why she wanted to probe so deeply.

'The results of my work speak for themselves.'

She couldn't deny that. Beyond his military and academic accolades, Zak Montegova had made a name for himself with his family trust. Had rivalled and in some ways elevated his family name more than his semi-reclusive brother had.

But then Remi Montegova's loss of his fiancée had resulted in his withdrawal from the social scene and the world in general, leaving his mother and brother to become the face of the royal house.

Had that put extra pressure on Zak? Was that why he held himself so stoically? Or was that ingrained in him for another reason? Realising she was back to dwelling much too long on the enigmatic man and not enough on her professional role, Violet turned away.

Only to have her elbow snagged in a firm hold. 'The bush might look harmless but be careful about wandering too close to it. Stick to the designated paths. You don't know what's lurking in there.'

Right at that moment she was more worried about the heat singeing her whole being from his touch than bugs or snakes. 'If I spend all my time worrying about what will jump out at me from the bushes, I'll never enjoy my surroundings.'

Peter heard her response as he re-joined them and nodded his approval. 'That's the spirit.'

Zak sent him a chilled glance that had the man's smile evaporating. Muttering an excuse about checking on their luggage, Peter left again.

'You're not here to enjoy yourself. You're here to work. Taking unnecessary precautions could end up inconveniencing others,' Zak declared.

He was right. And yet his retort stung deep. 'That's the difference between us, Your Highness. I give myself permission to enjoy my work. And by the way, I hadn't forgotten why I was here but, thanks, I'll bear your concern in mind.'

'You'll do more than that. I can't afford to have my schedule disrupted because of carelessness.'

She fought the urge to roll her eyes. 'I've just got here. I haven't had time to be careless!'

His gaze flicked pointedly to the hat on her head. 'Haven't you?'

She snatched it off and held it out to him. 'I'm not as fragile as you'd like to think I am. Besides, the worst of the heat is over.'

He didn't reclaim the hat. Instead, he conducted a slow scrutiny of her body.

By the time his gaze returned to her face, she was hot and tingly all over, and it had nothing to do with the blaze of the late afternoon sun or the trail of sticky sweat meandering its way down her spine.

'When was the last time you applied sunscreen?' he rasped, his voice a shade deeper.

She couldn't remember. 'I'm not doing this with you. I'm a grown woman capable of taking care of myself. Find someone else to snarl at.'

They'd circled back to where they'd left the vehicles and Violet saw with relief that their luggage was being unloaded. She seized the opportunity to wrest herself away from Zak's all-encompassing, disturbing presence. 'I'm going to unpack. If we don't have anything else to discuss, I'll see you in the morning.'

'You'll see me in an hour and a half, when we meet for dinner to go over the schedule for tomorrow,' he said silkily, but with that stamp of authority that said he expected his command to be obeyed.

Unable to resist, she glanced over her shoulder at him. Dark grey eyes regarded her steadily with a hint of challenge.

Violet resisted the urge to grind her teeth, reminding herself for the umpteenth time that he was her boss. He was calling the shots. For the next few months he virtually held her professional life in his hands.

Despite repeating all of that to herself, her temper still simmered by the time she reached the area where the tents had been erected on the east side of the site. She spotted Zak's immediately since it was quite impossible to miss. It was the largest structure, set away from the rest of the tents on its own little hill. Plus the presence of two bodyguards guarding the entrance gave it away.

'Miss?' The volunteer who'd been escorting her had stopped several feet from her, drawing her attention from Zak's imposing tent. 'Your tent is this way.' He indicated the path that went past the row of empty tents set a short distance away.

Frowning, she followed, her breath growing shorter the closer they got to Zak's tent. Surely he wasn't expecting her to share a tent with him?

'I thought I'd be using one of these smaller tents,' she said, aware her voice had grown husky and uneven. Hell, even a touch agitated. All at the thought of sharing a tent with Zak?

Yes.

No matter how much she tried to dice it, she recognised that exposure to him would fray what composure she'd managed to secure around him.

'You are,' the volunteer said, pointing to a medium sized tent tucked behind Zak's and away from the smaller ones down the hill. 'Well, it's kind of small,' he amended at her frown. 'But you're sharing Prince Zak's shower, not sharing with everyone else down the hill, so that's a bonus, right?'

Violet refused to examine the twinge that lanced her midriff at the realisation that she wasn't sharing a tent with Zak. Part disappointment, part relief? She pushed the emotion aside and thanked the man, who propped her large backpack in front of the tent and left.

She dragged her luggage inside and looked around. A small desk and chair had been set up on one side, with a carafe of water and glasses on a tray. The single bed on the other side held a surprisingly comfortable mattress and beside it was a nightstand on which sat a small but powerful lamp. At the foot of the bed was a shelved cabinet and a wash basin.

Simple. Rustic. A world removed from the opulent Park Avenue offices of the Royal House of Montegova Trust and the glitz and glamour of the fundraising ballroom in New York. And even the country manor house her mother had moved heaven and earth to cling to despite their questionable financial circumstances.

Yet Violet felt a sense of rightness and homecoming as she set her case down to unpack. Done minutes later, she set up her laptop on the desk, checked her emails—thanks to the newly installed Wi-Fi system—and ensured there were no last-minute emergencies to deal with before re-checking the volunteer roster.

Then, because her roiling emotions needed sorting through, she lay down on the bed, her gaze fixed on the apex of the tent.

Zak Montegova was here and was staying for the duration of the project. She needed to get used to seeing him every day. As long as she maintained professional distance, she had nothing to worry about.

A few short weeks. That was all she needed to endure Zak's presence...

Violet jerked awake, the realisation that she'd fallen asleep filling her with mild horror. A quick check on her phone showed she was ten minutes from being late to dinner. So much for her lofty assertion that she wasn't tired.

She flew to the cabinet holding her clothes, selected a white T-shirt, khaki shorts and brown espadrilles. Washing as best she could in the basin, she changed her clothes, brushed and tied back her hair.

She stepped out of her tent and stumbled to a halt. 'Oh, my God,' she murmured, awed by the sight before her. The cloud was awash with bursts of orange, greys and indigos. The hues were so powerful and spectacular she lost the ability to breathe as she stared at the stunning sunset. Thoughts of being late melted away, the sheer beauty of her surroundings holding her firmly in place.

'Is this your first?' a deep voice asked.

She hadn't heard Zak approach. Her stomach dipped alarmingly at the hushed gruffness in his tone. It was almost as if he didn't want to ruin the moment with their earlier animosity. She didn't want to look at him, fearing he would only add to the dramatic enchantment around her. But the sheer magnetism of the man drew her attention from the magnificent sky and sunset blazing over the lake, and she glanced at him to find his stormy gaze wholly fixed on her.

Heart thumping, she tried to recall what he'd asked her. 'My first?'

He turned away, presenting her with his haughty and perfect profile. 'African sunset.'

'I... Yes,' she whispered, a little afraid that speaking too loudly would make the glorious vision disappear.

The smallest hint of a smile tilted his lips, but it disappeared far too soon. 'It has the ability to evoke weak-kneed reactions.'

She stemmed the wild urge to ask him about *his* first. Had he been alone? If not, with whom? It was none of her business. So why the next words tripped from her lips, she would never know. 'I find it hard to believe you're capable of getting weak-kneed about anything.'

Did he tense just then? Thinking it wasn't wise to investigate too closely, and dying for another hit of magnificence, she turned back to the view.

But then he replied, 'If I didn't know better, I'd think you were feeling me out, Violet. Are you?'

She opened her mouth to deny it, but the words stuck in her throat. Did she want a demonstration of Zak's passion? Did she want to hear that deep voice murmur her name in that lightly accented timbre that slipped into his speech every now and then? Heat rushed through her, concentrating in her breasts and between her thighs as the power of his scrutiny singed her. Layer upon layer of sensation swelled, attempting to bury every precaution she'd recited to herself in the tent before sleep had overtaken her.

'Because if you truly are, you only need to say the word,' he added silkily.

Then she knew he was toying with her. Again.

It was there in the smoky mockery lurking in his eyes. There in the enthralling loose-limbed stance with in he held himself. But there was something else. Something ferocious that made her heart pound. That same intensity she'd spotted right before the ball, had sworn to stay away from because it was too dangerous but was now tempting her to peer into, brush her fingers against to test its true risk.

He shifted, turned to fully face her, as if offering her the very thing she needed to resist.

Her throat dried as the power of his masculinity threatened to knock her over. 'I don't need a demonstration, thanks,' she blurted, almost too afraid of the tingling in her body as his gaze lanced over her. 'I'll let you practise your dubious skills on some other unsuspecting female.'

She stepped away from him but not before she heard his low laughter.

Far from thinking he'd received the message, Zak fell into step beside her, his long-limbed stride shortening to match hers. Violet clenched her fists, freshly helpless against what the scent of rugged man and aftershave did to her insides.

'I don't dally with unsuspecting females, *cara.* Every woman who's graced my bed knows exactly what they're getting.'

She stopped abruptly, the images he once again evoked wreaking havoc of the jealous, unpleasant kind with her equilibrium. 'You shouldn't take everything I say as a challenge.'

'Ah, but then you have a unique way of saying things that makes me believe there's more, always more you're actually not quite saying,' he murmured, his gaze conducting that skin-tingling scrutiny of her face that left her feeling exposed.

Sensually vulnerable.

'How am I doing that, exactly?'

He stepped closer, filling every corner of her vision with his presence. 'It's your eyes, *dolcella*. You have the most expressive eyes I've ever seen. And unfortunately for you, they're in constant conflict with the words coming out of your mouth.'

His gaze dropped to her mouth and the rush intensified until her whole body was on fire. 'You either have an overactive imagination or you insist on seeing things that are simply not there.'

'Do I? I guess we'll make the discovery as to whether I'm right or wrong together.'

'We'll do nothing of the sort. They only thing we'll do together is—'

'Go to dinner?' he supplied, more with amusement than with his customary mockery.

Violet wasn't sure why his humour, even at her expense, eased and lightened something inside her. Made her almost…pleased to have been the source of his mirth.

This was totally insane.

'There you go again, *cara*,' he murmured. 'Your innermost thoughts blaze almost as fierce as this sunset.'

She forced a shrug. 'You believe you know what makes me tick. Perhaps I'm wondering the same about you. It's natural curiosity that I'm unsure it's worth fully indulging. That's all this is.'

An edgy little smile twitched at his lips, but he waved her forward with a smooth elegance that proclaimed his royal status. 'Then let's go and eat. Perhaps by the time we're done, you'll have decided one way or the other.'

She wanted to ask him why he was taking an interest. But then that would be prolonging this...*exploration*. So, while she would've enjoyed lingering for a little while longer to watch fiery day blend into star-filled night, she headed for the large tent designated for meals and gatherings.

The scent of sausages, grilled meats and fish assailed her nose as she entered, sparking a growling in her stomach that reminded her that she'd barely touched her lunch.

She was aware of heads turning their way as she and Zak headed for the food table, just as she was aware that the interest was all for him. Helping herself to small portions of local dishes, fried plantains, *ugali*, a thick maize porridge, and sauce, and a sausage on a stick while Zak chatted with Peter, she chose a seat at the end of the long banquet-style table. This was supposed to be a working dinner, and she didn't want things to veer off course again, so she activated her small tablet as soon as Zak joined her.

An email alert brought her up short. She clicked it, her heart sinking when she read the message.

'Problem?' Zak's deep voice rolled over her.

She bit her lip, loath to start their meeting by confessing a setback. But there was no avoiding it. 'Two of the volunteers have pulled out. One has an urgent family matter she needs to deal with, and the other's changed his mind. I won't be able to get replacements for a few days.'

'How are you going to fix that?' There was no challenge in his tone, only simple expectation.

'I'm going to move a few people around, ensure there's an even spread of skillsets to cover until the new volunteers arrive. And I guess this is where my general dogsbody role comes in handy. I'll lend a hand where needed until the replacements get here.'

He nodded. 'I'll do the same. You and I can make up the shortfall.'

Something snagged in her midriff, robbing her of breath

for a moment. 'You'll be helping to build lodges?' she asked, frowning. 'You... I wasn't made aware of that.'

'Would it have changed any part of your role?'

Yes, she would've been better prepared.

Before she could answer, he continued, 'I designed the lodges and worked closely with the company that developed them in Montegova. I'm best suited to step in more than anyone else at short notice. Even you, Violet.'

When it came right down to it, she couldn't object. This was his project, his name on the letterhead. It would've been easy to dismiss him if he'd been a spoilt, pampered prince, obsessed with his looks and getting his picture in the tabloids at every opportunity. But he was offering a sound solution to what could be an irritating setback.

'If you're sure...'

'I'm sure, Violet.' At her continued hesitancy, that edgy gleam returned to his eyes. One brow slowly rose. 'Unless there's another reason for your objection?' he drawled.

Aware that the table had grown quiet, she firmed her resolve and shook her head. 'Absolutely not.'

'Good. Welcome to my team.'

The emphasis on *my* ignited that blaze between them again. She held his gaze for as long as she could withstand the flame, then focused on her tablet, aware that once again she'd been outplayed, had slid that much closer to the edge of an abyss whose depths she couldn't quite fathom.

CHAPTER FOUR

VIOLET GAVE UP tossing and turning at five a.m.

She yearned to blame her restlessness on the different time zone and environment. But she knew the prospect of not only being in Zak's presence but the steel trap of working closely with him for however long he intended to remain here was the reason she'd lain wide awake for long stretches of the night.

Showered and dressed within half an hour, she headed to the food tent, where the local construction crew and skeleton volunteer staff were gathered. She spotted Peter the moment she entered and joined him after getting her breakfast.

'Good morning,' he greeted with a wide smile, pulling out a chair for her. His scrutiny was quick but appreciative, exhibiting harmless male interest a polar opposite from the kind she was used to. The kind her mother keenly invited constantly in a bid to find her and her sisters the 'right' husband. Refusal to accommodate their mother was the reason her twin sister, Sage, had taken a job on the other side of the world in New Zealand and rarely visited Barringhall these days.

She glanced up as Zak stepped into the tent, immediately sucking up all the oxygen from the space and directing more female gazes to him.

For the first time since she'd known him, Zak was dressed at his most casual. Yet even the expensive light-coloured cargo pants and white T-shirt shrieked their exclusivity. Although she suspected that dressed in rags, he'd somehow find a way to exude effortless sophistication and suave elegance. With his broad shoulders, potent good looks and dark hair that gleamed damply from his recent shower, it was near impossible to look away from him as he sauntered over to where she sat.

His grey gaze went from her almost empty plate to her half-finished coffee. Unlike Peter's, his scrutiny triggered fireworks in her body before it met her eyes. *'Buon giorno,'* he said, his deep, raspy voice making her skin tingle even more. 'I didn't expect you to be up this early.'

She shrugged, aware of Peter's interest in the exchange. 'I couldn't sleep so I thought I'd make an early start. The quicker I acclimatise to the routine, the quicker I'll shake off the jet-lag. Besides, the volunteers and trucks should be arriving soon.' And as soon as she rid herself of this disturbing reaction to Zak's presence, she could focus her excitement elsewhere.

'That's the best part—when the long wait is over and we get to see the structures actually going up,' Peter enthused.

Violet smiled at him, his effervescence infecting her.

'Let's hope all that enthusiasm doesn't suffer in the face of hard work,' Zak drawled, folding powerful arms across a wide chest.

She swallowed against the electrifying effect of his muscled biceps and glanced away.

Peter frowned, then shrugged. 'Everyone flags a little when faced with the scale of the work to be done but the ultimate goal is what pushes us all on. It's why I love what I do.'

Violet couldn't help but respond to his infectious attitude. She was still smiling when a female volunteer hurried over with a fresh pot of coffee and offered Zak a cup. For an infinitesimal moment, he didn't respond. His gaze remained locked on Violet a touch longer before he gave an abrupt nod.

Perhaps it was a good thing he was in a disgruntled

mood. It kept her mind from wandering into dangerous territory. Allowed her to steer her attention back to Peter.

'How long have you been in the tourism industry?' she asked him.

'I've never really done anything else. I started off as a tour guide and volunteer, then joined the tourism board to find ways to help the rural areas like these find ways to sustain themselves. It's in my blood,' he said with a grin. 'My Norwegian mother met my Tanzanian father on her gap year volunteering at an animal sanctuary in Dodoma. I was born a year after she finished her veterinary studies. When the opportunity came up to join forces with Zak's and tourist board's vision, I couldn't jump on board fast enough.'

The sound of large engines ended the conversation. The arrival of the volunteers was followed an hour later by excited shouts announcing the arrival of the eco lodges.

Excitement and a keen desire to please the Royal Prince kept everyone on their toes all though the first day. Violet allocated tents and assisted where she could, all the while ensuring she kept a safe distance from Zak.

That plan shattered when he approached where she was filling water bottles to distribute to volunteers. 'You were supposed to join me at lodge two after lunch,' he said, his shoulder brushing hers as he joined her to watch the last of the lodges being laid out in front of their designated sites.

She shifted away from him, her insides a little too jumpy and tingly at even that tiny contact. 'I'd planned to, right after I did this.' She started to lift the tray of bottles but he beat her to it, brushing her aside to balance the tray on one hand as he stared down at her with a fierce smoulder.

'Avoiding me isn't going to work with this thing you're fighting. You know that, don't you?' he rasped.

Despite her stomach hollowing out, she lifted her chin, daringly met his gaze and attempted to bluff her way through it. 'Since I don't know what you're talking about, I'm not equipped to give you an accurate answer.'

He stepped closer to make his point because surely a man like him didn't give a little damn about being over-heard? 'I'm talking about the fact that you're attracted to me, Violet. Have been for quite a while. The fact that you've been attempting to deny it. And the fact that your every action simply emphasises your naughty little dilemma.'

Should she bother denying it? Or should she confront it head on? Would the former merely attract further mock-ery because the evidence of it had lain like an unexploded firework between them since she'd made the mistake of throwing herself at him six years ago?

With a deep breath that failed to steady her, she chose the second option. 'So what if I am? You're decent enough to look at, and since you seem intent on alluding to my lapse in judgement six years ago, yes, we kissed, and, yes, that was halfway decent enough too. But let's not make a moun-tain out a molehill, shall we?' She wanted to fist pump for sounding convincingly nonchalant.

'Decent enough?' he echoed, something close to aston-ishment blazing in his eyes.

'Did you expect a higher rating? My memory isn't that great about the whole thing so you'll have to accept my generous verdict,' she said.

A circumspect gaze raked over her face. 'You have more fire than I remember. Fire I can't help but be tempted to stoke, to test the veracity of your claim. Perhaps even re-fresh your flawed memory.'

That sizzling need to throw herself into his particular fire blazed higher. She fought it with every shred of com-posure she could find. 'You're not going to get the chance. I don't particularly care to repeat the performance. Now, are we going to deliver this water or waste time recount-ing insignificant incidents?'

A long pause followed by an enigmatic smile was all she received in answer before he pivoted and walked away with her tray. With no choice but to follow, Violet gritted her teeth and did just that. Of course, with his help, the job took half the time, meaning that within minutes he was striding purposefully towards their designated lodge, where the team was waiting for Zak's signal to start.

His switch from sensually mocking into efficient commander was stunning and a little intimidating to witness. God, he would've been even more formidable in his military days.

Even more?

She shivered, drawing back from imagining Zak Montegova's jaw-dropping body in uniform, those lips issuing commands and talented hands manning the controls of the fighter jets he used to fly—

'Are you planning on joining in?' he drawled.

She focused to find the small group looking her way, one gaze in particular transmitting his knowledge of exactly what she'd been thinking about.

Aware of the faint blush staining her cheeks, Violet pursed her lips and strode over, avoiding Zak's gaze as she tore into the first pack. Luckily, he didn't comment further on her lapse of concentration and fell back into instructor mode.

Once she and the volunteers understood the basic instructions on how to construct an eco-lodge, the time flew by. Violet grimaced at the ruthless efficiency with which Zak worked, the fact that he worked harder than most on even the most mundane task in a fraction of the time it took for the rest of the volunteers to achieve the same result.

She wanted to resent him for yet another skill, but the sensation that burned within her every time she allowed her gaze to stray towards him was…admiration.

He wasn't afraid to put his mouth where his money was

and relished leading by example. Of course, when sweat and the heat of the day resulted in Zak pulling off his T-shirt and tossing it aside to reveal a hard-packed, flawless and gleaming torso that rippled and enticed with every moment, she especially despised the fact that she couldn't keep her gaze on her work, that her mouth watered and flames blazed deeper in that aching place between her thighs.

While his complete focus was on his task, unaware of or ignoring her stolen glances, which disgruntled her even more.

By sundown, the outer shell of their lodge had been erected and the primary emotion as she and the team felt as they took in the fruits of their labour beneath another spectacular sky awash with streaks of purple, red and orange was immense pride.

She joined the exodus towards the food tent, conscious that a shirtless Zak walked a few paces behind. Knowing the battle to keep her gaze off him would be harder, she lingered after she dished out her food until he was seated. Then she took the seat farthest away from him.

Peter joined her minutes later. But even as she kept a fairly easy conversation flowing, she was aware of Zak's growing scowl from the end of the long table. Aware that the presence of the other man next to her irritated the enigmatic Prince.

Too bad.

Perhaps it might do his ego some good to know that she wasn't one of the many females falling over themselves to hang onto his every word! With that wicked thought in mind, she laughed a little more enthusiastically at Peter's jokes, met his gaze a little longer and didn't object when he offered to walk her back to her tent, via the long way by the lake.

And when he bade her a perfectly gentlemanly good-night, she retreated inside with a smile, ignoring the little

dissatisfied hollow in her stomach as she gathered her toi-
letries and headed back out to take a shower.

While she was all for the luxury of a proper bathroom
and conveniences, Violet couldn't fault the special and simple delight of showering under the Tanzanian sky after sunset. The simple pump system delivered fresh water via a
shower head and she sighed with pleasure as the cool water
washed away the day's grime.

Of course all that delight turned to chagrin when she realised she'd forgotten her towel. With no choice but to stuff
her underwear into her wash bag and don her shorts and
T-shirt, she re-dressed as quickly as her damp skin would
allow and stepped out.

Directly into the path of Zak Montegova, leaning against
a slim acacia tree, clad in only a towel.

He straightened at the sight of her, sauntering over with
a mouth-drying swagger that made her every nerve ending
jump to attention. Dear God, how was it fair for one man
to be this attractive?

'For a minute there I wondered whether I'd need to take
a dip in the lake, in case you decided to use up all the
water,' he said.

She made a vague gesture towards the half-full pump
to the side of the shower stall. 'As you can see, I didn't.
There's more than enough for you.'

He kept his gaze trained on her, not deigning to glance
at the pump. And with each second she grew even more
aware of her dripping hair, of the T-shirt sticking to her
stomach and breasts, outlining her stiffening nipples. Of the
heat gathering between her thighs when his gaze dropped
down her body.

Had his breathing altered? Did that naked chest expand
as he sucked in a long breath?

Get yourself together!

She started to turn away, keen to heed her screeching senses.

'A word of advice, Violet. Whatever it is you're up to with Awadhi, be sure it's a choice you won't eventually regret.'

Was he cautioning her as her boss? Or was this... personal? 'You have a say in the work that I do. I don't believe you have a say in how I spend my free time.'

'Are you attracted to him?' he pressed, a definite bite to his voice. 'Can't get enough of all that wholesome, salt-of-the-earth, tie-dyed goodness? Is that it?' he mocked.

'Why? Are you jealous?' she taunted, exhaustion, a sense of injustice from being the butt of his cynicism and, yes, that constant, overwhelming need to give into the sizzling temptation he evoked just by *breathing* finally cracking her composure.

His nostrils flared. 'That would imply he has something that I do not.'

That stung deep, made her even more rash. 'If you're not interested then why are we having this conversation?'

He stepped closer, bringing his tower of virile masculinity and solid potency far too close. Her mouth dried and her fist clenched with the need to touch. To explore. To taste.

'You misunderstand me. The issue isn't what I want. It's what he doesn't have. Which is you. Because I won't allow it.'

Shocked, hollow laughter ripped from her throat, thankfully eroding a layer of need. *'Won't allow?* You have a nerve! Who do you think you are, telling me what you will or won't—?'

The rest of her inflamed accusation evaporated as he speared his fingers into her wet hair and drew her abruptly against his body. Hot, demanding lips slanted over hers, his arm banding her waist. He picked her up as if she weighed nothing, took three long strides and before she could take a breath she was plastered against the side of the shower stall, out of view of passers-by.

Zak held her immobile, angling her head as his tongue delved between her lips to begin a torrid little dance that instantly beaded her nipples, driving sharp, sweet pain between her thighs.

Violet had far too often relived their encounter six years ago, wondered if her recollections had been exaggerated because of the occasion, wondered if her childish crush on him was what had heightened her emotions.

This re-introduction was so much more than she remembered, her senses stunned anew as he expertly nipped her lower lip with his teeth and fresh, explosive sensation spiralled through her.

Perhaps she was older, hungry enough to appreciate him better, to savour this raw, intoxicating contact that had her questioning her sanity in allowing it one minute, then straining onto tiptoe, her arms trailing delightedly up those muscled biceps she'd admired to lock around his neck.

Whatever.

Caution evaporated away as she threw herself into kiss, tentatively nipping in return.

Zak made a hungry, greedy sound under his breath, muttered words in Montegovan she only half understood. Words that would've made her blush had she not craved it, yearned for satiation of the hunger growing inside her, demanding gratification.

She strained against him as Zak freed her mouth to explore the newly discovered erogenous zone beneath one ear. She shivered and gasped, clung tighter as he trailed his lips down her throat to her collarbone, then lower to one hard nipple.

His mouth surrounded the peak, taking flesh and cotton in one powerful pull. One hand slipped beneath the hem of her shorts to boldly cup her naked bottom.

Flames lit up her veins, pooling in a torrent between her legs. She gasped as, keeping their gazes locked, he moved his hand purposefully between her thighs, his fingers intent on one destination.

He absorbed her reaction, hungrily devoured her every shiver. With it came a speculative gleam in his eyes as he traced the heat suffusing her face.

'No bra, and no panties. I'm not sure whether to spank your naughty little bottom for exhibiting yourself like this or accept this gift you seem intent on giving me,' he growled against her lips.

Violet cried out as his fingers caressed her damp heat, breached her outer lips to rest against the soaked entrance of her womanhood. The hot brand of his own arousal jerked against her stomach as he absorbed her reaction, hungrily devoured her every shiver.

'Is it my touch that excites you like this, Violet, or the thought of being spanked, I wonder?' he rasped in a low, deep voice that strummed and deepened her need.

Frankly, Violet suspected it was both. And the more the thought seeped into her consciousness, the shorter her already compromised breathing grew.

Dear God, was she kinky on top of all her unwelcome woes?

Zak laughed beneath his breath, clearly witnessing her freaked-out expression. But slowly his laughter died, leaving a deeper carnal intent on his face. 'Is there something you wish to tell me, Violet?'

'I don't know what you're talking about,' she gasped.

'Don't you? You react too strongly to such an ordinary pleasure.' He squeezed her bottom again, kneading her flesh while boldly holding her gaze. 'You're all but hovering on the brink of orgasm from just this simple touch alone.'

He slanted his lips over hers once more, his tongue brazen, positively possessive as it slid against hers, determined to draw an even more potent reaction from her. Reaction she was helpless to deny as hunger clawed through her, wrenching her onto tiptoe again so she could taste more, drown more, *feel* more.

But that dim light of warning at the back of her head brightened, steadily but surely, slowing her reaction enough for her to pull back. A little too late she recalled what had happened the last time she'd allowed herself to give in to this sensation. He'd rejected her.

Nothing had changed.

Except this time she would reject him first. The last thing she wanted was to spend the next few weeks drowning in humiliation if he repeated the experience.

So, gathering the dregs of her composure, she bunched her fists against his shoulders. And pushed.

He growled beneath his breath for a second before he allowed her to break the kiss. 'Violet—'

'I don't care what you think. I don't want this.'

'Define *this*,' he insisted, narrowed gaze fixed on her wet lips for a tight moment before it rose to spear hers.

'Any…all of it. I'm not interested in scratching whatever itch you may have. Now or ever.'

'Such dire, sweeping pronouncements. Are you certain it won't come back to bite you?'

She took a step back, then another since one wasn't enough. His gaze dropped to her chest, landed precisely on one beaded nipple before switching to the other. And stayed.

Violet wished she could halt her agitated breathing. Wished she could stop her flesh from reacting to the ravenous hunger in his eyes. But he'd rejected her once and become entrenched in whatever dire opinions he had of her and her family ever since.

Falling into his bed would be as good as confirming

everything he'd accused her of. And she wouldn't be jeop-ardising just her body but the career she'd set her heart on.

'Yes. I'm one hundred per cent certain I don't want you to touch me.'

Dark rebellion glinted in his eyes but his words were smooth and immediate. 'Very well. You have my word I will not touch you until you ask...*no*, until you beg me to.'

Alarm strangled her lungs.

Why did that feel very much like a challenge?

And as she watched him walk into the shower without a backward glance, why did she feel like he was simply bid-ing his time until he *won*?

What the hell had he been thinking, making that prediction?

Five days had passed since their torrid little encounter by his shower. Five days of hell when either she plotted to drive him out of his mind or the little witch cast a spell on him.

Zak swiped an arm across his sweaty forehead and stepped back to survey another excellent day's result. They'd shaved a whole day off their target, building two eco lodges in five days instead of six.

He didn't apologise for being a harsh taskmaster when the occasion demanded, and the high fives happening be-hind him suggested the team didn't mind, either.

Violet's husky laugh made his stomach clench tight.

He didn't want to turn around. Didn't want to be drawn to her attention-absorbing face, her supple, curvy body or those control-wrecking legs she insisted on displaying in the bottom-moulding shorts she favoured.

As for her work ethic...

Contrary to his dim prognosis, she'd delved into every task with wholehearted enthusiasm, more often than not going over and above expectations. Not once had she protested.

Of course, he still had his reservations that she could sustain it in the long run—

A choking cough shattered his thoughts and intentions. He turned and found Violet doubled over, the subject of the team's humour as she spluttered.

'A little warning next time, please?' She laughed through the coughing.

Zak's gaze narrowed at the volunteer holding the suspicious-looking bottle as he approached, unable to take his eyes off Violet's legs and plump, shapely behind as she bent over to cough again. The reason for her state became apparent when he caught the scent.

Pombe, the local alcoholic brew, was lethal to the unschooled. 'What do you think you're doing?' he demanded.

Everyone froze, their gazes avoiding his.

'We're celebrating. What does it look like?' Violet responded, the humour dying from her eyes.

'Perhaps you should consider celebrating with something a little less…potent?' he suggested.

While the rest of the team sent him wary glances, Violet shot him a challenge-filled glare. All week she'd treated him to those defiant little looks. Having grown up in a Royal household where most people fell over themselves in deference and yearned to please, Zak found her attitude… uniquely interesting. Perhaps a little too much? Was that why he couldn't resist needling her whenever the opportunity arose?

He shoved the suggestion away when her chin lifted.

'Where's the fun in that?' she taunted, her eyes still shiny from her coughing episode.

Perhaps it was frustration. Perhaps it was disgruntlement that she wouldn't fit into the mould he'd cast for her. Before he could stop himself, his fingers were wrapping around her forearm. 'For those of you who prefer it, I've had champagne delivered to the tent to celebrate finishing early. Feel free to go and help yourselves,' he said to the group.

Predictably, his announcement was met with a chorus of cheers and the team dispersed quickly.

'Would you please stop manhandling me?' she sniped as soon as they were alone.

He released her but planted himself in front of her. 'How much of that did you drink?'

'Policing my activities yet again?'

'Only in the sense that you're inviting a hell of a hangover by indulging in that stuff.'

She swiped the back of her hand across her lips, dragging his attention back to the full, luscious mouth he'd tasted. The mouth he couldn't get out of his head. 'Thanks for your concern but that's my problem, surely? Have I done anything so far to compromise my work?'

He pursed his lips. 'Not yet, but there's always a first time.'

A flash of emotion, possibly hurt, darted across her face. 'And you're, what, positioning yourself as my champion? To save me from myself? Why?'

'Because we're leaving tomorrow. And I'd prefer you to be at your best, not hung over and jet-lagged when we return to New York.'

Her alluring eyes widened, right before she frowned. 'We're leaving? But we've only been here a week.'

Considering the words spilling from his lips were a surprise to him as well, he absorbed the astonishment well, he thought. Congratulated himself on the inspired thinking, even. 'Do you think there's something more you can learn by remaining here?' he countered.

She bit her lip. 'No, I'm sure I can put together an eco-lodge in my sleep now. But I thought we...that *I* was staying to see this project through.'

'I've changed my mind. Why waste more time here when you can gain more experience on the next project?'

He could tell she was torn between the need to argue and the need to accept the carrot he was dangling. 'Where are we going next?'

Zak shrugged. 'I have to return to Montegova at the end of the month. Until then, my itinerary is fluid but it doesn't lack requests for my presence at various projects. Who knows, perhaps I'll let you pick the next destination.'

She turned away, casting a longing look over the site and the surrounding landscape. 'This is a beautiful place. I was looking forward to my half-day off tomorrow to explore.'

Another spur-of-the-moment thought hit him. 'You'll have to make do with a visit to the phase two site, provided you can be ready to go immediately?'

She faced him again, surprise reflected in her eyes. 'I… Of course.' She looked down at her stained and work-worn clothes. 'Give me a few minutes to change and clean up and I'll join you.'

He shook his head, a stab of impatience driving him harder. 'You're not attending a red carpet event, Violet. You're fine as you are. You can shower when we get back. Or, if you insist, there's a lake you can use to wash up when we get to the site.'

Mutiny rose in her eyes and Zak's muscles tightened, anticipation flowing through him at the thought of tussling further with her. But she tossed her head and with a shrug waved a hand at him. 'Fine. Let's go.'

She headed towards the area where the vehicles were parked. Zak let her go while he issued quick instructions to his bodyguard. The guard nodded and sprinted into action.

'How long is the drive?' she asked when he reached her.

'Normally an hour, but we're not driving. We're taking the chopper. Come.'

The pregnant chef had been evacuated two days previously at the first signs of her labour, reducing the likelihood that the aircraft would be needed in the next few hours.

When they reached it, he held the door open for her, unable to resist glancing at her smooth bare legs as she slid into the seat. Her eyes widened when he took the pilot's seat, leaving three of his bodyguards in the main cabin.

'You're flying this thing?' she asked, tentatively taking the headset from him.

He didn't miss her scepticism. 'Courtesy of a full licence from the air force, I'm quite capable of it, Violet. No need to be afraid.'

He was gratified to see the scepticism melt from her eyes, although he wasn't quite sure how long his groin would sustain the pressure at the sight of her breasts outlined by the dissection of the seat belt.

He was still debating the wisdom of this tour when he lifted off and headed east.

Through the mic attached to the headset, Zak heard her soft gasp as he set down ten minutes later on the flat landscape near the edge of Lake Lengai. Once again Tanzania was showing off its jaw-dropping beauty with another stunning sunset but this time against the backdrop of a cascading waterfall thundering into a shallow pool that fed into the lake below.

He'd chosen this spot for phase two primarily for the ready fresh-water source, but watching Violet dart from the chopper, unabashed joy on her face as she raced towards the waterfall, Zak took a reluctant beat to see the land through her eyes, to appreciate the beauty of his surroundings.

When he joined her, she was straightening from leaning down to run her fingers through the clear water. 'It's...beyond spectacular,' she said a touch reverently, a lot mournfully.

'Your tone suggests differently.'

'Because the pool is shallow and wildlife-free. I would've brought a swimsuit with me if I'd known.'

Immediately, his brain supplied him with a vivid picture of her clad in a bikini. He shifted, almost growling at his body's eager response.

His shrug was a masterclass in fabricated calm. 'We're both adults, Violet. Unless you're once again naked beneath those shorts and T-shirt, you can improvise.'

In the fading light, colour washed her cheeks, strumming an elusive thought that faded before he could grasp it. 'That's none of your business. Shall we get on with the tour?'

The tour took fifteen minutes, and again she asked pertinent questions, her thoughtful observations backing her conduct on the project so far.

It didn't prove anything, he told himself.

Her mother was equally as passionate about landing a fat cat for her daughter, preferably one with a title and bottomless wallet. All this…passion could be a carefully orchestrated plan.

Just like the general's nearly successful strategy in those crucial and terrifying days after his father's death. Just like the restless factions whose motives and whereabouts were still proving elusive to pinpoint in his homeland.

The reminder restored a little more calm, reasserting his sense and control. Enabled him to summon up appropriate dispassion when they returned to the edge of the lake, where his bodyguards, following his instructions, had set up their evening meal.

He walked past a frozen Violet to their picnic blanket. 'Are you going to just stand there all night or join me?'

Suspicion filled her eyes as she ventured closer. 'I… You set this up?'

'I thought we could kill two birds with one stone. The

likelihood that there'll be anything left to eat when we return is slim. Sit down, Violet.'

Four solar lamps were positioned on each corner of the picnic blanket, providing ambient light as darkness fell.

He watched her sink down, fold her long, shapely legs beneath her before plucking a grape from a bowl. 'You're a prince. Isn't it the done thing to summon a chef to prepare a meal from scratch if the fancy takes you?'

'Of course, just as it's this easy to arrange a picnic by a lake because I wish it.'

She'd fully expected him to deny her veiled insult, and he watched, amused, as she blushed again. He reached for the champagne bottle set in the ice bucket and worked the cork free, aware her gaze lingered on him.

'Something on your mind, Violet?'

'You mentioned your pilot's licence from the air force. Why did you leave the service?'

Because the man he'd been dying to impress, the man he'd looked up to and called Father, had died unexpectedly, shattering a secret dream and leaving a nightmare in his wake. Not only had his father not been the man he'd thought him to be, his weaknesses had left the kingdom he should've been safeguarding in jeopardy. Only by strengthening their foundations in the eyes of the world had they kept from toppling over into the abyss the King had left by his death.

Not a subject he was in the mood to revisit right now. 'I served my time until I realised I could better serve my kingdom in another role.'

'But, from that meeting with the minister, it looks like you're still in charge?'

'Some matters of national security will always fall within my remit, yes,' he said, aware his voice was clipped. He ended her questioning by popping the cork. She flinched but accepted the glass he passed her.

'You were in a celebratory mood earlier. No reason why you can't raise a toast to your achievements this week.'

'You say that with a straight face, yet your dry tone mocks the very thing I'm supposed to be celebrating.'

'Let's leave the analysis for now, Violet.'

'Because you don't like hearing the truth?'

'Because I'm famished and don't wish to invite indigestion.'

For the rest of the meal they ate in silence that drew far too much of his attention to her face, her body, the movement of her throat when she swallowed.

The moment they were done, she rose.

'Where are you going?'

She threw him another defiant glare as she walked away. 'To take a better look at the lake, after all. At the moment it's a little more appealing than the company.'

CHAPTER FIVE

He gave her five minutes while the remains of their picnic were tidied away. Then Zak approached the water.

Flames leapt in his bloodstream when he saw that she'd more than just taken a look. Her T-shirt and shorts were neatly folded on the grass near the water's edge and Violet was submerged up to her neck, her body turned from him as she performed unhurried breaststroke.

Without stopping to debate the wisdom of it, Zak tugged off his clothes and slipped into the water. The fresh water did nothing to cool the pounding in his groin as she sent him another glare over her shoulder, then purposefully increased the distance between them.

He wanted to breach it, wanted to truly explore why this woman got beneath his skin so effortlessly when every woman before her had failed to even crack his veneer.

He managed to resist the urge for as long as it took her to swim within metres of the waterfall.

'Are you going to avoid me all night?'

She gave a rich chuckle. 'Now, there's a thought worth serious consideration.'

Laughter spilled from his throat, surprising them both, if the slight widening of her eyes was an indication. 'Have I really been so fearsome?'

'Don't flatter yourself. You've been disagreeable, discourteous and downright rude, but you'll have to go a long way to be fearsome. To me at least. Can't speak for the masses.'

He raised his eyebrow at her list. 'I've been all of those things? How very trying for you.'

'Like I said, don't flatter yourself. I can more than handle you.'

The flames leapt higher. 'Can you really?'

She hesitated, her gaze meeting his for one bold moment before sliding away.

'How about we make a deal? For tonight only, you have my word that I'll be more…accommodating.'

That regained her attention. 'And what does that entail, pray tell, seeing as it'll be a complete novelty to me?'

He shrugged. 'I'll leave the testing of it up to you. But if you intend to interrogate me, I suggest you come closer. I don't wish to compete with the mighty waterfall for conversation.'

She glanced from him to the thundering waterfall, then swam in lazy, graceful strokes towards him until she was just beyond arm's length.

His fingers vibrated with the strongest urge to snatch her, plaster the body that had shattered every night's sleep since their arrival against his.

It took a monumental effort to resist the urge, to stay put as she eyed him with thinly veiled suspicion. His poker face must have passed muster because she ventured a shade closer. Until he could count every moonlit pearl-shaped drop on her flawless skin. Trace the fullness of her lower lip and watch the sensual sweep of her tongue lick away the droplets that clung to her soft flesh.

His fist bunched as need climbed higher. She saw his reaction and for a moment triumph flashed through her eyes. The foolish little witch… 'Has no one taught you it's unwise to play with fire?'

One shapely eyebrow lifted. 'All I'm doing is swimming, Zak. You're the one who seems to be…disturbed.'

Even as she said the word her nostrils fluttered, and he

was willing to bet the moonlight hid her blush. That innocent reaction triggered an even more urgent question.

'Do you have a boyfriend, Violet?' He suspected not, considering her mother's end goal, and the certainty that if mother and daughter's goals were aligned, they would be circumspect about publicising such a relationship. But that wasn't to say Violet, like any other matrimonially ambitious socialite, wouldn't seek to amuse herself along the way to landing herself a rich husband. The sudden need for confirmation intensified the longer she hesitated. She opened her mouth and he interrupted the heated rebuttal. 'Or a conveniently clandestine lover, willing to keep your bed warm until he's no longer of use to you?'

Expecting anger or even a heated denial, all he received was a withering look. 'This is you on your *accommodating* behaviour? What is it about me that chafes at you so badly you feel the need to keep picking at my character?'

For the first time in his life, Zak suffered the sting of... shame. He refused to give it another name, refused to consider that this form of attack spoke to a vulnerability in his own character.

'Or is it because you're unwilling to admit you're stumped when it comes to me?'

'Hardly.' He infused his tone with as much boredom as he could muster.

Head tilted, she regarded him with something close to... enlightenment. 'That's it, isn't it? All these weeks you've been expecting me to behave a certain way, confirm all your suspicions. And I'm not, am I?'

Those last words were uttered so softly the thunder of the waterfall almost snatched them away. But he heard them. Heard and refused to acknowledge even a fraction of them held any truth. He wasn't stumped. He simply needed more proof.

The last time he'd accepted anyone or anything at face

value, he and his family had paid a steep price. Shattered trust was a difficult thing to regain.

While Violet Barringhall may not represent a toppling of his family's throne or epitomise his personal anguish, Zak had learned not to give any quarter.

'Your mother has been hounding me with emails, demanding to know how her precious daughter is doing.'

She stiffened, her hands momentarily stilling in the water. 'What did you tell her?'

'Nothing, so far. She doesn't quite rate in my list of priorities. Not yet anyway.'

She tried to hide her relief by glancing away. Zak allowed her a moment's reprieve before he continued, 'That's not to say I won't send her the response she seems to crave. I was curious about one thing, though…'

Her gaze snapped back to his, apprehension flashing in her eyes. 'What?'

'Her continued insinuation that this project, you being out here, is all some sort of perfunctory exercise for you. A stepping stone to what you're really after.'

Again, emotion flashed in her eyes, frustration and perhaps even hurt. But she mastered her expression, a little too admirably. A different need hammered at him, one that wanted to see her…undone. Unfettered.

'If you think I'm going to dishonour my mother by maligning her just to prove a point, you'll be waiting a long time,' she snapped.

Loyalty. A quality he would've admired if not for the disturbing reactions teeming inside him. 'You want me to make up my mind one way or the other about you, then prove it.'

'I thought I already had this past week.'

'Work is work, and I've yet to make up my mind on that score. Like you said, this is personal. Prove that all this isn't some sort of tedious playing-hard-to-get game.'

Her beautiful eyes narrowed and she expelled a stunned breath. 'Reverse psychology? Really? What do you want? For me to prove I can indulge myself with you for a few minutes, then walk away instead of begging for a ring on my finger the way you believe I yearn to?'

The curiously husky note in her voice intensified the pressure in his groin. The scenario wasn't as deplorable to her as she pretended.

He smiled, the voice whispering at the back of his mind that he was enjoying this far too much ignored as he replied, 'It doesn't necessarily have to be a few minutes. A fraction of time to show me you can operate with no strings attached. An hour or two will suffice.'

She gasped, and this time he swore he saw the colour suffusing her face. Either the challenging Lady Barringhall was prone to blushing or her innocence was more than surface deep.

The hot coil of possessiveness and need was totally misplaced and deeply unwelcome. And yet there it was, sinking twin talons into him as he watched her alluring face.

'You want to kiss me as much I desire you to, Violet. There's no shame in admitting it,' he stated boldly. 'Or perhaps it's the begging part that worries you? Would it please you if I took that off the table too?'

She inhaled sharply. But despite her desire to cling to outrage, Zak read her interest loud and clear. Saw the way her gaze dropped to linger on his mouth before darting away. 'You can have any woman you want, according to the giddy tabloid headlines. Why are you here, needling me, *Your Highness*?'

Never had his title sounded so sultry, so insistently *arousing*, falling from a woman's lips. He wanted to hear her breathe it all over his skin, wanted her gasping it when he buried himself deep inside her.

His fists bunched beneath the water as the powerful

surge of need momentarily stunned him. 'I could never resist a challenge. Perhaps I wish to see how long you can truly hold out.'

Her eyes glinted and for a moment Zak feared he'd finally pushed her too far.

In the next moment, however, Violet tripped him up completely by slicing through the water. She came straight at him, one hand sliding up his nape to fist his wet hair while the other curled around his shoulder.

And because he absolutely didn't want to spook her into changing her mind, Zak held stone-still, watching a touch of confusion then resolution settle on her face. Held his breath as she levered herself closer, plastered her chest against his.

And slid her lips over his.

One moment. Two. Five excruciating seconds he managed to hold out.

Then he sealed her in his arms, glorying in the smooth, supple feel of her skin as he locked her to him and took over her far too tentative exploration.

She tasted even headier than before, the sensual slide of her tongue when he breached her sweet lips a lightning bolt to his system.

Dio, how was she doing this to him? Even as he tasted and savoured, his hunger built, threatening to shatter his control. A soft, throaty moan left her mouth. The sound curled around him, hardening his already rock-hard shaft.

She registered her effect on him, gasped against his lips as he groaned, and deepened the kiss until he was unsure where her body ended and his started.

Until only his lazy kicks kept them afloat.

Until Zak suspected nothing would douse the flames leaping within him save for the ultimate act. The thought staggered him, made him wonder if he was willing to take things that far.

Si, his charged libido insisted. She'd accepted his challenge.

Perhaps he needed to prove his own point, deliver a message to the Barringhalls and every grasping leech out there that the Montegovas weren't to be trifled with.

They were both consenting adults. Even if one of them exuded innocence that hinted she might be unschooled in some aspects of sex.

Again the thought sent a pulse of primitive possession smashing through him, even though he refused to believe it. Made his caresses bolder, hungrier as he cupped her breast and toyed mercilessly with the stiff peak. Her unfettered shiver and sharp cry drove him even further into insanity. Drowned him in the urge to devour her.

He growled in protest when her fingers slid out of his hair. About to command her to return them, to pull tighter... harder, he stopped when she dropped her hands to his shoulders. Anticipating more, Zak trailed his lips down her throat, tongued that leaping pulse he'd been thirsting for all evening. Gratified when she gave another delicious shudder.

Right before she altered her touch. The hands on his shoulders weren't caressing. They were insistently pushing him away. A little stunned, he watched her kick away from him. 'Is that enough for you? Are you convinced now?' she asked, her voice passion-husky but determined.

'No, I'm not. Because that wasn't enough, *mia bella*,' he growled, lunging forward to recapture her. Drag her close once more. 'Not nearly enough.'

Electrifying sensation threatened to douse the warning signs flashing through Violet's brain as Zak lowered his head. The thought of experiencing his explosive kiss once more, of feeling his tongue and teeth and lips saturate her senses made her whole body grow weak, wantonly needy.

It was a good thing he still held onto her or Violet was sure she'd be a useless lump at the bottom of the pool right now.

He drew closer still, his sensual lips a tempting whisper away.

Dear God, what was she doing?

Proving a point. But one that she'd already proven, surely?

Not nearly enough.

His words echoed in her head, louder, more insistent, eroding her common sense. Because he was right. That taste hadn't been nearly enough. All it'd done was rake over every dampener she'd put over her emotions and re-awakened them so rudely, so effortlessly it'd set her whole body on fire.

Now the very thought of walking, or swimming away, felt like an insurmountable task. One that would be made easier by giving in one more time?

She ignored the voice mocking her logic, made a noise that sounded suspiciously like a whimper when he held himself that last scant inch away. Ruthlessly teasing? Or perhaps as unsure as she was?

She ventured a glance into his eyes. And was met with blazing arousal that left her in no doubt that Zak was as into this as she was. Still, his lips brushed furtively over hers. Sizzling but way too brief.

With a helpless groan she sealed her lips to his once more, ignoring his grunt of pure male satisfaction.

Just once more. One more minute and she'd end this insanity.

They strained against one another, determined to best each other in this battle of wills and kisses that required a victor. When the hot steel rod of his arousal imprinted itself against her belly, she whimpered some more, a driven urge to touch him, stroke him driving her hand beneath the water.

At her first touch, he tore his lips from hers. Eyes dark and mysterious in the failing light raked over her face. At first, Violet thought the thundering in her ears would surely deafen her. Until she realised they'd swum right up to the waterfall.

She blinked against the drops pelting her face, gasped softly when Zak's large hand framed her jaw, tilted her head upward to meet her gaze. Without releasing her, the arm banding her waist lifted her onto one flat boulder.

He moved between her legs, ferocious intent in his eyes.

She wanted to compare this moment to those in her mother's garden six years ago, but Violet knew she couldn't.

For one thing, the cool reserve lurking in his eyes then was nowhere in sight now. The hands trailing up her knees to frame her hips were possessive, purposeful enough to convince her that he wasn't about to stop any time soon. That unless she stopped it this time, Zak was fully intent on accepting whatever she gave.

His gaze dropped from hers to trail a fiery path down her throat to the agitated rise and fall of her breasts. One hand moved from her hip, up her ribcage to rest beneath one breast. Momentarily freed from his gaze, she glanced around her.

He'd set her down on a flat boulder large enough to recline on, solid enough to take both their weight. And with the thundering waterfall now shielding them from the outside world, it seemed like the perfect place for a seduction.

Was this what he'd intended all along?

Her heartbeat tripled as she stared at him. Whatever words she was cobbling together to ask him, they dried in her throat as his thumb grazed one tight nipple, his gaze riveted on her face, absorbing her every reaction.

Another pass and she shuddered, biting back a moan.

'You like that?' he rasped.

Violet caught her lower lip between her teeth, absurdly

reluctant to admit she did despite the blatant evidence he couldn't miss. A twist of his lips told her he had his answer and was perhaps content to let her off the hook.

In the next instant his other hand joined in the torture, moulding the twin globe until she couldn't help the tight cry that fell from her lips.

After an electrifying minute, he started to draw back the wet fabric of her bra. And at last she found a shred of common sense. 'Your guards—'

He shook his head. 'They won't disturb us. Their job is less about watching me and more about watching out for potential threats.'

Her privacy protest battered away, she was confronted with another question that loomed large in her mind.

Was this really happening?

'Should I be pleased or insulted to be excluded from that scenario?' The question was a throwaway one, meant to buy her time to regroup and rebalance, but she was nowhere near sane, shuddering as he caught her flesh between his thumb and forefinger and squeezed.

Expecting a rapier-sharp comeback, perhaps even desperate for one to restore her sanity, Violet was mildly stunned when his face grew dark and dangerous. 'Any misjudgement will be down to me. Not them.'

She couldn't help but wonder if there was a hidden meaning behind his words. A meaning she herself needed to heed before it was too late. 'Zak—'

'I believe that's the first time you've used my name. Say it again, Violet.'

'Why?'

Expert fingers caught her chin, angling her face so he could better scour her expression with his electric gaze. 'Because I find my name on your lips…pleasurable.'

'Zak.'

Ferocious eyes spiked into hers. 'I want to taste you,' he

announced, his voice hot, raspy, setting fire to her pelvis. 'Stop me now if you don't wish this to continue, Violet.'

She opened her mouth intending to do exactly that or at the very least slow down this relentless freight train of passion threatening to run away with her. At the last moment her throat closed up. Was this a turning point? Or was this her opportunity to draw a line under what had started six years ago?

She'd spent long endless nights craving more of that brief taste of desire. Now he was offering her a feast on a platter. Wasn't he? She searched his gaze, eager to discover whether this was another prelude to a rejection. She found only a fierce hunger that matched her own.

But hadn't he looked the same that night too?

Sensing her reticence, Zak dropped his hands from her body and rested them on the rock beside her hips, holding her in place just with the look in his eyes. 'Don't overthink this. What happens here stays here, Violet.'

'You mean in the light of day we forget that this ever happened?' Why did that press on a tender spot in her chest?

He shrugged. 'If that is what you wish. What it will not be is a pretence that what happens between us here will lead to something more. That is not on the table.'

Why not? she wanted to ask, but she already knew the answer deep in her bones. Something more would never include the likes of her. She only needed to glance at his family history to see the sort of pedigree the Montegovas chose to have lengthy relationships with.

Remi had been engaged to a woman with a flawless background, despite her commoner status, and their mother was a renowned ex-beauty queen, coming from a prestigious family and an heiress before she'd married the King.

Even now, the Crown Prince was said to be hunting for a woman of impeccable pedigree to replace his dead fiancée. Violet was sure nowhere on that list was a minor aristocrat with a background soiled with near bankruptcy, disgrace and a tabloid-hungry mother who sold gossip on a regular basis.

'This isn't a world-altering decision,' he insisted.

But in a way it was to her. A few mind-blowing kisses were one thing but giving herself to Zak Montegova completely was quite another.

And just like that the issue of her virginity loomed large before her eyes. She bit her lip, nerves eating fresh at her as she contemplated how to break the news to him. Perhaps he would be turned off, just as he had been by her awkward crush on him six years ago. Was she better off keeping it to herself?

'You want me,' he insisted, his tone deep and fierce, angling his mouthwatering body closer.

'I'm not denying that.'

'Then what is this about?'

His eyes gradually grew icy as he stared at her. 'You didn't answer me before. Is there someone else? Is that why you hesitate?'

A wave of anger swept over her. 'You really think I would be here doing this with you if I was in another relationship? What sort of women do you date?'

He barely flinched at her accusation. 'While I'm inclined to think that heated response answers my question, I don't wish to assume. Is there someone else, Violet?' he demanded again, his voice terse.

'No, there isn't. I haven't had the time or the inclination to do…this or have a relationship. Of any kind,' she added, just so he would understand she was including whatever schemes he believed she was hatching with her mother.

'I have an understanding with my liaisons and I've set out what my expectations are.' He stopped, his eyes heatedly scouring her body before returning to hers. 'I despise deceit. So this is your chance to end this or give me your answer.' He brought his body another tempting inch closer. 'If you want me, touch me.'

The invitation was too much to resist.

In that moment, Violet knew she'd passed the point of no return. As for her virginity, one way or the other he would find out that she was truly innocent soon enough.

Even if he didn't realise it, after this she only needed to proceed as normal for a few more months. Then she would be out of this life. Why that thought sent a lance of pain through her chest, she refused to examine.

She would take this moment out of time, slay the dragon of need that'd consumed her for so long and then put it all behind her. Then she could go on with her life.

'*Dio mio*, do I really need to beg?' he demanded roughly.

'Perhaps you do. Perhaps I want to see that unique event,' she teased.

A smile twisted his lips, but it was the raw need in his eyes that threatened to stop her breath. A feeling of urgency rose inside her, and without waiting to see whether he would actually resort to begging, she hooked her fingers behind his neck.

The blaze of triumph in his eyes should have made her hesitate, but all Violet could think of was that her fierce hunger was about to be sated.

He delivered a hard, consuming kiss to her lips, and every thought melted from her brain. The tasting was over in an instant and then his lips were trailing down her neck again. This time his destination was purposeful as he caressed the skin with one hand while his other eased in a downward trajectory to one breast.

He lightly bit the plump slope, causing her to cry out again. Before the sound died, he was wrapping his lips around one tight peak. He licked, tortured and delivered heady sensation the likes of which Violet had never experienced. Flames flared from the point of contact through-out her body, coalescing in that tight space between her legs and making her hips jerk and strain with the need for satisfaction.

Because this was Zak, because he was effortlessly at-tuned to her needs, he didn't leave her waiting for long. Taut fingers trailed over the sensitive skin of her belly be-fore stopping at the boundary of her panties.

Bold and brazen, his fingers delved beneath the wet fabric. Her breath strangled in her throat. She hung on the edge, every molecule in her body strained at the twin points of contact.

And then his finger slipped between her folds, igniting raw, acute pleasure through her veins. Her head dropped back on her shoulders, the effort to keep herself upright weakening as Zak spread her knees wider, sought better access.

Access she couldn't deny him as her craving escalated.

He caressed her swollen flesh, growling in satisfaction as he encountered the slick evidence of her need. In raspy Montegovan, he muttered against her nipple, the sound lost in the thundering waterfall but no less arousing. For endless minutes he toyed with her while swirling his tongue around one nipple until need gathered unbearably in her pelvis.

'Zak…'

He laid her back against the rock, dragged down the straps of her bra and bared her breasts to his eyes. Then he drew back, taking his time to conduct a sizzling scrutiny of her body. '*Madonna mia*, you are exquisite,' he breathed.

Flames of lust lit through her at his words, her reaction pleasing him, if the turbulence in his eyes was any indi-cation. He returned to his attention to her breast, catching the sensitive flesh between his teeth as his fingers delved deeper between her thighs. He breached her core, growling a torrent of Montegovan when he encountered even more evidence of her need.

Slippery, hot, ready, he caressed her expertly before pressing one finger to her core. Violet tensed momentarily. It wasn't enough to change her mind but the knowledge that this was actually happening was enough to attract fresh nervousness.

'So tight. So snug. It's almost enough to make me wonder if you're untouched,' he said.

Here's your chance. Tell him.

She didn't know why she held back or why she dropped her gaze instead to watch the magic he was evoking between her legs. The sight of the carnal, erotic caress made her whimper.

His head surged up. 'Violet? Is there something you wish to tell me?'

She swallowed, then dredged up the keenest poker face she could muster. 'Is this a Q&A or are we going to get on with it?' she asked boldly.

His gaze raked her face, narrow eyes probing hers. Violet undulated her body, straining closer to his touch. She wasn't aware her nails dug into his shoulder until he relaxed and gave a low laugh.

'Is my little hellcat impatient?'

'You're the one who seems to have all the answers. What do you think?'

Without answering, he sucked one nipple into his mouth, and then the other, groaning at her fresh shudder before licking the space between the globes.

She lost the ability to string thoughts together, falling backwards on one elbow as he charted a path down her midriff to her navel and then lower.

Aware of what he intended to do, Violet was torn between stopping him and going with the flow. 'Please...'

He lifted his head, speared her with those intense grey eyes. 'Will you give me what I want, Violet?' he rasped.

'And what's that?' she whispered.

'To taste you. Here,' he said, running his knuckles over her heated core.

She cried out. He gave a harsh exhalation, dispensed with the teasing and tormenting, lifted her hips off the rock and sealed his mouth to her aching body.

Sensation like she'd never known rushed through her. Her body twisted and jerked as Zach boldly explored her. Her clitoris became his plaything, her centre his playground as he took his time to deliver pleasure heaped upon pleasure.

Eyes squeezed shut, Violet could only ride the wave as paradise beckoned. She was vaguely aware of tiny screams ejecting from her throat, of cool water lapping against her shoulders and the hot solid column of Zak's body positioned between her legs. Everything else ceased to matter as her climax gathered with fierce concentration between her legs. And when that moment came, when with a bold caress he shoved her off that peak, she screamed, certain she would never be the same again as every cell exploded in ecstasy.

For endless minutes she floated, almost afraid to open her eyes, afraid to discover if this had just been another lurid dream. Even though none of her dreams had ever felt this earth-shattering.

Violet opened her eyes, her heart lurching when she was confronted with the solid reality of Zak in his full magnificence, totally focused on her.

She understood at that moment why women went crazy for this man. If what he'd done to her moments ago was even a fraction of the pleasure he could deliver, then every flick of his arrogant eyebrow and every word that fell from his lips in utter self-confidence was justified.

Not that she was about to tell him any of that. His ego didn't need the boost from her.

Certainly not in the manhood stakes, she thought in stunned wonder at her first glimpse of his arousal. At some point between laying her down on the rock and gifting her that mind-blowing orgasm, Zak had removed his boxers. Unashamedly naked and magnificently virile, he held himself over her, making room for himself between her thighs.

The faintest flicker of uncertainty slid through her mind. Could she accommodate him? Perhaps he spotted it. One corner of his mouth lifted in a tense little smile. He lowered his head and brought his lips to hers, his tongue easily breaching her lips to commence a slow gliding dance that evoked what he intended to do to her.

Apprehension melted away but a warning tweaked the back of her mind. It evaporated when he settled his mouth-watering body against hers, leaving her gasping as every erogenous zone in her body roared to life.

'Look at me, Violet,' he urged, his gaze fusing with hers when she raised her eyes to his. 'Touch me,' he commanded.

All along she'd fooled herself into thinking that this was simply an experience to indulge in and move on. But even before he had settled his hard length against her core, Violet suspected that this was so much more.

'I want to see your eyes as I take you,' he said, his voice deep, profound, soul-stirring enough to make her tremble with something more than pleasure.

Too much. It was too much.

Thoughts loomed large and impossibly momentous in her mind as Zak surged inside her, filling her up, breaking through that final barrier of her innocence.

He froze, shock filming his eyes and slackening his jaw as he stared down at her with something close to icy condemnation and searing regret.

CHAPTER SIX

'MOTHER OF GOD. You're untouched?'

Violet struggled to breathe, struggled to drag her mind from the sensations ricocheting through her body. The initial sting of his penetration had receded fast to leave behind a wild hunger that demanded fulfilment. Hunger she was immediately terrified he wouldn't sate as he started to withdraw.

'Please.'

Zak shook his head once, a tight, shaken expression still on his face as he glanced down at where they were still joined and then up to meet her gaze once more. 'Why didn't you tell me?'

'Does it matter?'

A rough sound barked from his throat. 'You think it didn't?'

'Perhaps I didn't want to make a big deal out of it.'

He started to pull back even further. She clamped her legs around his waist, somehow believing that would stop him. Miraculously it did, fresh tension shadowing his face as he paused. 'It is a big deal, Violet.'

'Why?' she asked, then winced inwardly. Dear God, was she really having this discussion with him? Right now?

Shock and a touch of bewilderment washed over his face. 'You really think me so callous that I wouldn't have minded whether you were innocent or not?'

She clamped her legs tighter. He shuddered, his body falling forward as he groaned. 'It's already done, Zak. Let's not overthink it.'

For the first time in her life she spotted indecision on his face. It made her bolder, the thought that here, now, her femininity was more powerful than his resistance, sending a wave of triumph through her. 'You wanted to take me. Well, here I am,' she dared.

With a torn grunt, he surged forward, driving the last dregs of apprehension away and filling her with searing pleasure. One stroke. Two. On the third stroke, Violet was introduced to a new platform of sensation that made her jaw drop. Whatever came next, she was sure that this sublime feeling would never be surpassed.

'Why, even now when I know I should be stopping this, can't I end this thing?' he groaned almost under his breath, his bewildered gaze dancing over her face. The gleam morphed, turning deeper. Possessive.

Why that infused her with even more pleasure, Violet didn't want to pause to examine. Emboldened, she spiked her fingers through his hair, raking her nails over his scalp the way she'd tested at some point and discovered he liked. He shuddered, his eyes glinting in the dark as he stared at her.

'You're determined to bewitch me, aren't you?'

'Am I? Then why am I being denied?'

He sucked in a harsh breath, his chest expanding, dragging it against her nipples. They both shuddered. She undulated, that peculiar need surging high as her body demanded more. Zak thrust inside her one more time.

From then on no words were necessary. The slide of hands, the stroking of tongues, the slippery penetration transmitted need and propelled her towards another earth-shattering climax.

Violet was almost afraid that she would be wholly consumed by the depth of her pleasure, so much so she tightened her grip on him, attaching every part of her body to his solid frame, revelling in the deep shudders that racked his frame as he found his own climax. Eventually the tide receded, hearts slowed, reality intruded, leaving behind a slow-cooling lava of alarm that hollowed her stomach.

Because while throwing caution to the wind had been freeing and eye-opening in the pleasure stakes, she was terrified that she may have given a whole lot more than she had intended to.

Even now as Zak withdrew from her and turned to swim a few feet away, she wanted to grab him and pull him back, beg him for more of what he'd just given her. Like her distress as he'd taken up her thoughts and invaded her dreams for the last six years, with this experience she was suddenly terrified there would be none other like the man who had just taken her virginity.

There was no such profundity on his face when he tugged on his boxers and faced her, however. Just grim-faced shock.

'Violet,' he rasped, his voice ashen with something close to horror. 'I didn't use any protection.' Regret and fierce condemnation drove away pleasure as reality smashed into her brain.

Oh, my God.

How could she have been so reckless?

He needed a moment to think. Scratch that. He needed several moments.

A week. A *month.*

Perhaps a stint in an asylum because only that would explain what he'd just done. His error of judgement came rushing back in a torrent wilder than the waterfall thundering behind him.

He'd taken her innocence.

Even while that admission sent another spike of primitive possessiveness through him, Zach was reeling from how he'd spectacularly compounded the severity of the situation.

He'd not only taken her, he'd taken her innocence without protection.

Dio mio.

He'd handed her everything she needed to destroy him. He wasn't a wet-behind-the-ears schoolboy, so how could he have been so monumentally stupid? Acrid bitterness wove through him, enough to make him bunch his fists as he sorted through his shaken thoughts. Was this what had driven his father, too? Desire so strong common sense had ceased to exist?

Unwilling to dwell on his father right now, he returned to Violet.

The women he usually slept with had two modes of post-coital interactions—sultry invitations for a repeat performance or, more usually, a gentle probing as to how soon they could once again grace his presence.

One look at her showed Violet was far from exhibiting either of those cloying signs. If anything, she was in a tearing hurry to dress, her movements clumsy as she secured her bra and panties.

Momentarily arrested by her beauty and disarmed by the thought of never experiencing sex with her again, it took a moment to realise she was glaring at him.

'If you're worried this is some scheme to trap you, don't. I'm on the Pill.'

The relief he should've felt was…minimal, stunning him anew at his actions tonight. He shuddered to think what else would surprise him.

He'd never dared a woman into sleeping with him, for starters.

When several indicators had pointed to her innocence, he'd still forged ahead. He gritted his teeth at the unfortunate pun, instantly reminded of her snug, mind-melting heat.

'Why am I surprised that you're freezing me out?' she accused. 'Everything you said was a lie, wasn't it?' she threw at him, refocused, affront coating every word.

'I don't believe I've even uttered a word,' he returned, attempting to gather the control that'd shattered into a million pieces.

'Believe me, your body language speaks volumes.'

'And what is it saying exactly that has you so riled up?'

Dark blue eyes sparked flames at him. 'Don't patronise me. What happened to "what happens between us stays between us"?'

He shrugged. 'Have I done anything to indicate otherwise?'

'You're not already wondering if this wasn't some sort of trick that I performed on you?'

Since he'd thought exactly that, and he wasn't about to admit it, he merely shrugged.

'You're unbelievable.'

'You said you're on the Pill. I'll return the favour by saying you have nothing to risk healthwise from being with me. But your overly emotional reaction is…concerning.'

His icy delivery stopped her cold. Her eyes widened with apprehension as she stared at him.

'Whatever happens after this please promise me that this isn't when you decide to pay me back for what we both indulged in by ruining my life. My work is the most important thing in my life.'

Fresh shock unravelled through him. Did she really think him that callous? 'I gave you my word and I intend to keep it.'

For a moment after she'd slid off the rock and stepped into the water, she searched his features.

Zak wanted to lower his gaze, evade whatever it was that she was looking for. Because he wasn't thinking straight. Probably hadn't since he'd got into the helicopter to come here.

Slowly, he let the ruthlessness his ancestors were renowned for, the ruthlessness some had accused him of, fill his veins.

What was done was done.

He'd slept with Violet Barringhall, despite his intention to stay away from temptation. He still craved her, if truth be told. Even now as she determinedly swam away from him and surged out of the lake towards where she had left the rest of her clothes, he couldn't drag his eyes away from her curvaceous body.

But that didn't matter.

There was no point wishing she was anyone but who she was, a risky venture he should never have tangled with. As he followed, his mind raced through every pitfall that could arise from this. By the time he boarded his helicopter again, he knew only one option was open to him and that was to ensure this never happened again.

Because contrary to what he had so loftily attempted to deny, Violet had almost come within a whisker of sliding beneath his guard, creating havoc.

He didn't intend for it to happen again.

Two months later

Violet stood up shakily along with the cathedral full of the *crème de la crème* of European royalty, a Russian oligarch or six, and wall-to-wall dignitaries and celebrities. In unison, they watched the wide doors of the Duomo di Montegova, the sixteenth-century cathedral located on its own picturesque hill in Montegova's capital, Playagova, to catch a first glimpse of the bride as she slowly made her way down the aisle.

While she made a pretence of being agog, her mind was

far away, spinning wildly enough to give a whirling dervish a run for its money.

She wished she could stop thinking about everything that'd happened since that night in Tanzania. At least then her head wouldn't spin so hard she feared she would pass out.

Fists discreetly clenched, she fought through the sensation. Under no circumstances could she break down here, now. Her mother's eagle eyes would zero in on her and Margot would demand an explanation of what she'd termed 'Violet's odd behaviour' in the past few days. Violet could only thank goodness her twin sister Sage had flatly refused to attend, and her older sister Charlotte, who'd held a secret flame for the Crown Prince, had been too morose at the announcement of Remi's marriage to notice Violet's less than radiant appearance.

No, she couldn't give in to the hysteria bubbling beneath her skin.

She definitely couldn't give in to tears. She'd succumbed to them a few times already, and these days it seemed as if tears waited around the corner, ready to exploit any unsuspecting emotion she succumbed to.

So she plastered a smile on her face, turned towards the advancing bride, hoping that her make-up would cover the worst of the shadows that had gleefully mocked her when she'd looked in the mirror that morning.

Thank God she'd declined her mother's invitation to share a suite at the five-star hotel they'd been booked into for their stay in Montegova.

And thank God her mother was too busy lamenting the fact that Crown Prince Remi had slipped through her clutches, eliminating himself as suitor for her older daughter, to pay closer attention to Violet.

As she'd been doing for the last few weeks, her mother would spend most of her time gossiping and giving her opinion about the longevity of the upcoming nuptials, freeing Violet to wallow in her misery.

Violet didn't have an opinion one way or the other. She'd only seen the bride, Maddie Myers, very briefly at the pre-wedding party thrown by the Queen two nights before, and Violet would be the first to admit that she hadn't been at her best that evening either.

But then who could blame her?

You only have yourself to blame, the voice that had been haranguing her endlessly insisted. Recalling her behaviour that night at the waterfall, she felt the blood drain from her face. Weeks later, she could barely believe that had been her.

How she'd wrapped her thighs around him and urged him on. How she'd flaunted her rock-solid contraception in his face afterwards and promised he had nothing to worry about.

How very wrong she'd been.

Wrong and completely compromised.

She'd stopped bothering to decipher the ins and outs of how the contraception that was meant to be reliable had failed her. All she knew was that it had, and the promise she'd given now needed to be taken back. Because the very thing he'd feared had happened.

She was pregnant with Zak Montegova's child.

An incontrovertible fact that had the power to render her speechless every time she thought of it. And she'd had a lot of time to think about it ever since her period had failed to make an appearance.

'Ah, here's Zak now,' her mother said, anticipation throbbing in her voice. Completely unaware of the fresh barrage of shock she'd just delivered to her daughter.

Heart banging against her ribs, she followed her mother's gaze.

Zak was escorting the bride, the confident half-smile

aimed at Maddie sending discreet sighs throughout the cathedral.

Violet wasn't one of swooning crowd. Been there, done that. The consequence of it was growing inside her this very minute. Nevertheless, she couldn't help but gaze at the stunning image he made in his impeccable best man's suit.

In the weeks since she'd last seen him, he'd stayed true to his word and given her nothing to worry about in the work stakes. What he'd failed to mention the morning after their night by the waterfall when they'd boarded his private jet back to New York was that his way of ensuring nothing would adversely affect their working relationship was to remove himself completely from any interaction with her.

Because no sooner had they arrived back in New York than he'd absented himself from the House of Montegova Trust, and departed for parts unknown.

She'd been left with more than enough to occupy her, had even gained much-needed experience on other projects, sent detailed reports to Zak after every completed task. But he'd neither acknowledged them nor made a re-appearance in the New York office, leaving her with nothing but time to absorb the earth-shattering confirmation that she was pregnant.

With Zak's baby.

Steeling herself against a fresh barrage of bewilderment, she attempted to drag her gaze from him as he neared, to hide herself behind elaborate fascinators and wedding hats.

But, with the accuracy of a guided missile, his head swivelled towards her, dark and stormy grey eyes singling her out of the crowd. The smile he'd been sharing with his soon-to-be sister-in-law evaporated. And perhaps she was deluding herself, seeing what she wanted to see, but Violet could have sworn he stumbled as he saw her.

Of course, that wasn't true.

Her mother was godmother to his older brother. Her name was on the guest list.

And if neither of those facts had registered and suggested the possibility of her attendance, Violet had sent him emails, requesting a meeting with him, none of which he'd unanswered.

Leaving her with no choice but to succumb to her mother's pressure to attend this wedding. She may not have been ready in any way for the news she now bore, but neither did she want to keep it from him.

It didn't matter that she suspected he would treat it with even more of that icy disdain he was showing her now. It couldn't be helped.

He was the father of her child and he deserved to know. Once she'd delivered the news, she could get down to the reality of how she would work her life around a child.

Her child.

Her hand crept towards her flat belly, as it'd been wont to do with terrifying frequency and a stunned joy these past few days. Sucking in a breath, she hastily dropped her hand. She needed to remain on her guard before her mother spotted the tell-tale sign.

The last thing she needed was her mother's opportunistic interest ratcheting up the pressure that was inevitably heading her way now that Remi was off the market.

As if intuiting her thoughts, her mother turned towards her. 'Be sure to find Zak and have him confirm that he'll be writing you that letter of recommendation. I don't really see the point of why you would go to such lengths to do the work and not capitalise on it.'

Violet bit the inside of her cheek to stop herself from responding. She would be hunting Zak down but not to pursue the letter of recommendation. At least, not immediately.

While she needed the letter, it wasn't her priority at the moment.

Besides, she had no right to the letter, not when she still had weeks left on her secondment contract.

She composed her expression when her mother sent her a sidelong look, turned to face forward and silently prayed for the time to whizz by so she could leave Montegova.

Her mother believed she was staying on for the post-wedding festivities planned by the Queen but Violet had changed her ticket for an earlier flight out of Montegova tomorrow. In all the scenarios she'd cast through her mind of how Zak would react to the news, she didn't believe it would include an invitation to celebrate at the Royal Palace. Hell, he would probably throw her out of his kingdom himself.

'Violet?' her mother demanded under her breath, her eyes narrowing.

God, she really needed to get herself under control.

'The bride looks stunning, doesn't she?' she said hurriedly, momentarily distracting her mother.

The ceremony began in earnest then, thankfully excusing her from conversation. Drowning in her own thoughts, Violet barely registered the ceremony. She offered congratulations when she needed to, smiled during the photographs afterwards and before she knew it she was being whisked into the jaw-dropping ballroom in the equally magnificent Montegovan Royal Palace.

Throughout the long speeches and the long line to offer congratulations to the Crown Prince and his new Princess, Violet was aware of Zak's overshadowing presence. Just as she was aware that he was ignoring her.

More, she was painfully aware of the single socialites gravitating towards him with a sickening covetousness that set her teeth on edge.

She told herself she was irritated simply because his engagement with other guests was eating into the time she needed to tell him her news and make her exit. But the excuse rang hollow inside her.

Because, as she'd predicted that night after they've made love, he'd invaded her thoughts even more insidiously than he had six years ago. It was as if now she'd experienced true passion, it...*he'd* imprinted himself indelibly on her psyche. His absence from New York had sharpened her hunger, intensified it exponentially. So much so that even when she promised she wouldn't glance his way now, her gaze defied her will, seeking him out as he danced with one stunning woman after another, exchanged laughs with his brother and courteously escorted his mother around the ballroom.

Knowing she needed to get herself under control if she was to remain level-headed for their upcoming meeting, Violet excused herself and made a beeline for the cloak-room. Retouching her make-up and taking several deep breaths lowered her heart rate by a laughable fraction, but beggars couldn't be choosers.

Neither could they afford to linger interminably in the cloakroom.

Passing shaky hands over her dark peach floor-length gown, she headed for the door, a half-smile plastered on her face. The smile dissolved to nothing when she opened the door to find her elusive Prince framed in the doorway.

No.

He wasn't *her* elusive Prince. He was simply the elusive man who'd treated her like a pariah since taking her virginity. No, that wasn't wholly accurate either, her inner voice mocked. She'd been a willing participant in the act, urging him on when he'd attempted to put the brakes on their passion.

While she wasn't one to dwell on might-have-beens, Violet needed to face reality. And she needed to face it head on. With that in mind she angled her head to meet his gaze, even summoning that elusive smile to counter his mocking one.

'Hello, Zak.'

'For someone who's been feverishly chasing me, you don't seem particularly happy to see me,' he drawled, his lazy tone belying the fiery intensity in the gaze that raked her from head to toe and back again.

Her heart dropped. 'So you knew I was looking for you? And you didn't bother to return my emails or get in touch?'

His arrogant, dismissive shrug sent an arrow of hurt deep into her chest.

'The reports you sent regarding your projects were adequate enough not to require further discussion. Beyond that, I fail to see what you'd have to discuss with me. But seeing as you're making personal demands, I thought I should double check.'

She barely managed to stop her fist from clenching. 'I've been in Montegova for two days and at this wedding going on four hours,' she said, not bothering to hide her caustic tone. 'Are you making some sort of point by avoiding me?'

His gaze blatantly raked her again, lingering at the pulse racing at her throat before rising to meet hers once more. That intensity had risen, giving him an almost dangerous look. 'You look stunning, Violet.'

Flames lit through her blood. She attempted to ignore it. 'Don't change the subject.'

His jaw tightened. 'As I've said, your reports came in regularly and since nothing demanded my immediate attention, I drew my own conclusions as to why you were clamouring to see me.'

She refused to acknowledge the wild lurching of her heart. 'Which were?'

'That this demand is extremely personal. And since we discussed in detail how we wouldn't make personal demands of each other in the aftermath of our…coming together, I thought it wise to give you a chance to rethink this meeting. Obviously, you have no intention of doing so, so let's get this over with, shall we?' he drawled, his tone extremely bored.

'Wait, you think I'm gagging for more of the same?'

His eyes narrowed at her caustic tone. Then he caught her by the elbow.

Anyone who saw them would've believed he was escorting her but his firm hold told her otherwise. 'Where are you taking me?'

'Where the scene you seem to be intent on having will have minimal impact.'

Violet couldn't help herself, she laughed. 'You really are full of yourself, aren't you?'

He didn't respond, simply led her towards a set of double doors flanked by two uniformed sentries. With smooth precision, they opened the doors as Zak walked her through, and then closed them.

Despite having primed herself for this meeting, Violet was unprepared for the full impact of finding herself alone with Zak in a room that look like a smaller version of the one holding the wedding reception.

He hadn't changed much. There was a tautness about his jaw and his hair seemed a little bit longer, lending him an edgier aura of danger.

'I love a good appreciative scrutiny, but your timing leaves a lot to be desired,' he drawled.

'What are you talking about?'

'Maman has admonished me not to attract attention or gossip at my brother's wedding. Being locked in a room with an attractive woman isn't the best way to avoid it.'

Violet felt heat wash up her cheeks and devour her face. He wanted nothing to do with her. Wished no hint of their association to be broadcast. For a moment, she contemplated just turning around and walking out. Let him discover the news that his indiscretion had borne fruit in a little over seven months.

But even as she contemplated doing so, she remained rooted to the spot. She'd barely been able to sleep in the last few weeks. There was no way she could do this to herself any longer.

'Violet?' Her name was a terse command from his lips.

'Don't worry, Zak, I don't want to be here any more than you want me to be. But while I came to Montegova out of courtesy to your brother, I also did want to speak to you. And it has nothing to do with work.'

His eyes narrowed, suspicion growing with each second that passed between them. The blood rushed in her ears, the knowledge that once she released the words there would be no taking them back strangling her vocal cords.

'You wish me to fetch the string quartet, perhaps? Add a little suspenseful music to this dramatic performance?' he mocked.

'You may find all this amusing or boring or whatever emotion you're trying to project but, believe me, this is the last place I want to be.'

He tensed, his body solidifying to stone as he continued to watch her with an intensity that sent skitters of apprehension over her. 'Then make it fast.'

Simply because her heart was threatening to hammer itself out of existence, her head spinning with the effort of keeping herself under control, Violet exhaled and let the words fall from her lips. 'I'm pregnant.'

For the longest stretch of time he simply stared at her. Then his breath hissed in a sizzling exhalation. 'Repeat that,' he ordered.

'There's nothing wrong with your hearing, Zak. You heard me right the first time.'

Several emotions chased across his face, none of them calming her roiling senses. The ones she managed to decipher only accelerated her heartbeat, the shock at his discovery of her virginity in no way competing with the icy shock and anger that finally remained once he'd composed himself.

'You are not reckless enough to attempt to trick me so I'm going to take you at your word,' he rasped through flattened lips.

How she managed to locate her vocal cords to respond would remain a mystery to her. 'I won't thank you for that because I'm sure there's an insult in there somewhere. Facts are facts, though.'

His nostrils flared as his gaze dropped down to her belly, drawing her attention to that telling gesture that had once again taken her by surprise. This time her hand stayed, splayed over her stomach in a protective gesture. When his eyes rose to hers, Violet could tell he'd fully acknowledged it.

A moment later he pivoted away, reached into his pocket and extracted his phone.

He spoke too fast in Montegovan for her to decipher even the word or two she understood of the language she should've mastered a long time ago if only her mother hadn't pandered more to her English side. 'What are you doing?' she asked when he hung up.

'You know my family's history so you know I have a half-brother who was sprung on us the day of my father's funeral.'

She frowned. 'Yes. That isn't news, is it?' she replied, wondering where he was going with this. 'What does that have to do with—?'

'Very few people will ever know the depth of the chaos Jules's unexpected arrival caused in our lives. Like you, her mother chose a significant occasion to deliver her news.'

She gasped. 'Surely you don't think—'

He cut across her once more, his tone icier than ever. 'Believe me when I say that I'm not going to sit back and watch it all happen all over again.'

Her heart lurched at the intensity and determination in his voice. 'I don't understand.'

'You will,' he replied.

Heading for the door, he summoned one of the guards and returned to where she stood. 'You will watch her. Make sure she doesn't leave this room. Is that understood?'

The guard snapped to attention. 'Yes, of course, Your Highness.'

Violet rushed forward. 'Wait, what do you think you're—?'

He turned towards her, his face a mask of determination as his eyes speared into hers. 'Who else knows?' he demanded.

'I... No one.'

'For your sake I hope that's the truth.'

'I'm not a liar, Zak!'

Without acknowledging her response, he turned and started walking towards the door.

'Zak, if you think I'm going to be left here cooling my heels whilst you waltz off and do...whatever, know that it's not going to happen.'

He stopped, pivoted towards her without approaching. 'Tell me, Violet, was your intention in coming here to have a discussion with me?'

She slanted a glance at the guard, who stared into the middle distance, effectively mimicking a seen-but-not-heard stance most likely drummed into him as part of royal protocol training. Her gaze returned to Zak's. 'Yes.'

'My duties are mostly finished but I cannot carve out the time for this without first going back to make my excuses. You will wait here for me to return.'

'But—'

'Unless you've changed your mind about the supposed urgency of this situation?'

For the life of her, Violet couldn't see the web he was spinning even though silky threads whispered over her skin. She would've loved to flounce off after delivering the news, but she couldn't sustain any more shocks. Couldn't live in limbo as she tried to decrypt his full and eventual reaction to her pregnancy. She had to stay, see this through in order to better inform her next steps.

'But we don't have to do this right this minute, do we?'

'And when do you propose we do it? That we get together at another state occasion, perhaps?'

'That wasn't my fault. If you had bothered to answer my emails—'

He waved that away with a flick of his wrist. 'The past is past. I know what you have come to tell me now. And I am going to do something about it.'

She opened her mouth, but again he halted her speech with a slash of his hand. 'I'm willing to bet my mother has noticed my absence and is already sending someone to look for me as we speak. Do you wish me to handle this and come back to you or not?'

What could she say to that except, 'Yes. Okay.'

With an abrupt nod he walked out the door, leaving her with an icy dread she couldn't quite explain. A wave of dizziness rushed over her, and Violet stumbled over to the nearest set of sumptuous matching sofas and sank into the nearest seat. Scenarios raced through her mind as an hour ticked by without Zak returning. She had the absurd thought that he'd abandoned her, was circulating the ballroom, secretly laughing at the absurd news she'd delivered.

The doors opened and a second guard entered. Violet watched, a little bemused, as the two guards exchange a low-voiced conversation before advancing towards her.

'Would you come with me please, miss?' one said.

'Where are we going?' she demanded suspiciously.

'His Highness has requested that you meet him at a different location.'

Frowning, she glanced towards the double doors that led back to the wedding reception. 'But…my mother…'

Her words were met with a blank stare.

Aware that returning to the ballroom now would attract questions, Violet concluded it was wisest to get this meeting with Zak out of the way. Rising, she smoothed at her hand down her thighs and nodded at the guards. 'Lead the way.'

They led her away from where the reception was still in full swing, traversing a series of hallways until they emerged into an enclosed courtyard where a gleaming black unoccupied limousine stood idling. The back door was open with the driver poised at attention beside it.

She resisted the urge to ask the guards where the driver was taking her, suspecting that she'd be stonewalled. Sucking in a breath that did nothing to sustain or restore her equilibrium, Violet slid into the car and fought back a shiver as it was shut softly but precisely behind her.

The car rolled forward. Through tinted windows, she saw the palace grounds whizz past. Mourned the beautiful architecture and stunning city of Playagova she'd been too preoccupied to fully appreciate.

Within minutes they were pulling up to a building that looked suspiciously like an aircraft hangar. Her suspicions were confirmed when the car glided to a smooth stop next to a gleaming jet a size smaller than the one in which they'd flown to Tanzania.

Its tail fin bore the same royal logo. The driver opened the door, courteously holding out his hand. For a moment, Violet hesitated. Sensing she would get no answers from the driver either, she alighted, then watched in surprise as he rounded the bonnet, slid behind the wheel and drove off.

'Hey, where are you—?' Realising she was alone in the cavernous space, and that she was speaking to thin air, she turned and eyed the steps that led into the plane.

Apprehension eating at her, she climbed the stairs and

entered another sumptuous, custom-designed interior. Aged cherry wood complemented gold-veined marble in a masterful display of opulence that would have completely bowled her over had the sight of Zak, lounging in a large club chair at the far end of the plane, not absorbed every ounce of her attention. She approached him only because she didn't want to conduct this meeting by shouting the length of the plane, her feet moving soundlessly over the thick carpet. She stopped within ten feet, close enough to talk but not enough to be overwhelmed by his presence. *Much.*

'What is this, Zak? What am I doing here?'

He didn't immediately reply, instead looked past her and nodded.

Glancing sharply over a shoulder, Violet saw the pilot acknowledge Zak's silent command and retreat into the cockpit.

Only then did Zak address her. 'Sit down, Violet.'

She eyed the doorway, swallowing with relief to see it was still open. 'No. Not until you tell me what's going on.'

'I thought we could speak privately about your…news.'

'You can't say the words, can you?'

His gaze dropped again to her belly, a look slashing across his face but disappearing far too quickly for her to decipher. 'That you're pregnant? That you claim to be carrying my child?'

'Claim? I thought you said I'd be too reckless to pull the wool over your eyes with such a claim?'

'We'll get to the details of that in a moment. First, I really wish you would sit down.'

Two things pierced her consciousness simultaneously.

The first was that the engines of the plane had started up, the stairs electronically retracting until the door shut with a soft whoosh.

The second, as icy foreboding raced down her spine,

was the sight of the weekend bag that should've been in her hotel room sitting against an interior door of the plane.

The enormity of what was happening weakened her knees. Before she could collapse and disgrace herself, she sank into the nearest chair, which happened to be the one directly opposite him. He rose with lithe, efficient movements, secured her seat belt, then stayed put, crouched before her as if he expected her to jerk upright and sprint for the door. As she wildly wanted to do.

But already the jet was rolling forward, slowly gathering speed once it had left the hangar.

'What the hell do you think you're doing?' Her voice was nowhere as firm as she wanted it to be. Because she suspected she knew what was happening. Knew but refused to acknowledge it.

'You've been demanding my attention, *mia bella*. So I'm giving you what you want.'

CHAPTER SEVEN

ZAK STARED DOWN at the sleeping form of the woman who claimed to be carrying his child. He wanted to be amused at the hours of silent treatment she'd punished him with following his announcement, right before she'd just as silently taken him up on his offer of the master suite to rest.

He couldn't dredge up an ounce of humour.

He'd instructed his personal security chief to dig into every second of Violet's movements since their night in Tanzania. Preliminary reports indicated that besides work and being in her apartment in New York, she'd done little else.

No secret lover hovered in the wings, aiding her plot to deliver this bombshell into his life. Even communication with her own mother had been kept to a minimum, fuelling his impression from what he'd spotted of the strain between the two women during Remi's wedding reception that Violet was avoiding her own mother.

That notion had been confirmed when Margot Barringhall had, under the guise of congratulating the new royal couple, cornered Zak to demand if he knew what was up with her daughter.

If even her own mother didn't know…

He shook his head, knowing he was avoiding the main subject that need to be addressed. His feelings towards her news.

He was going to be a father.

Simultaneous waves of ice-cold shock and a red-hot need to claim thundered through him, as had been happening ever since Violet had made the life-changing announcement.

A child.

His heir.

He didn't regret the steps he was taking to ensure that no whiff of scandal accompanied this news. His mother's announcement that she was stepping down from the throne with immediate effect, together with his brother's imminent coronation, would be fodder for those who sought to take advantage of the changes going through the kingdom to further their own nefarious ends.

But kidnap? Really?

Si, he affirmed to himself. His actions were justified. As he had learned to his cost when his father had died, delaying in taking action could prove detrimental.

While she may have lapsed into mutinous silence following his announcement that he was in effect kidnapping her, he wasn't in any doubt that this was merely the calm before the storm.

Zak shoved his hands into pockets, refusing to acknowledge the act was to stop him from tracing his fingers down her smooth cheek, then running them through silky hair loosened by sleep. Long eyelashes curled against her paler than normal cheeks, her make-up having failed at its job of disguising the shadows under her eyes or the weariness turning down her sensual lips.

He'd spotted the signs of strain long before he'd approached her at the reception. Had spent far too long wondering if he'd overworked her.

He frowned, belatedly realising he hadn't asked after her health. How was she coping with the baby? Was his child the reason she looked so pale?

His child...

He exhaled long and hard, registering that with the passage of time the icy dread was receding, and in its place was an even greater clamour. One that demanded immediate and definitive resolution to her claim with a claiming of his own.

As if she could intuit his thoughts, she shifted in her sleep, angling her body away from him and cradling her belly with her right hand.

Another hard smile curled his lips.

Whether she knew and expected it or not, she'd sealed her fate by informing him that she carried his child. No Montegovan child born of the royal family had ever gone unclaimed. When his father's indiscretions had come home to roost, they'd been forced to accept his half-brother, despite Jules's existence creating chaos within the royal household.

Even the very thought of a small part of history repeating itself made him grit his teeth. He turned and strode to the nearest window. They were still hours away from landing at their final destination. He needed to return to his seat, ensure his plan was firmly in place.

But even as the thought rippled through his mind, he was looking over his shoulder at Violet as she tossed again in bed. For a moment he entertained the notion of joining her there.

Almost immediately he rejected the idea.

Temptation was what had led them here in the first place. Temptation was what had driven him to Australia for the last two months, pursuing his trust's interests on the other side of the world secure in the knowledge that she was on her way out of his life.

Except she hadn't been. And she couldn't have found a more permanent solution if she'd tried.

Bitterness twisted inside him. She'd well and truly pulled the wool over his eyes.

But no more.

If the child she carried was his—and he was still of the

opinion that she wouldn't dare to attempt to foist another man's baby on him—Violet would be left in no doubt that he fully intended to claim what was his.

That thought settled deep within him, finally erasing any doubt or apprehension about the course of action he was taking.

Slowly retracing his steps back to her, he paused long enough to pull the light coverlet over her body before he exited the master suite. Passing the sitting area, he made his way to the conference table on the lower deck of the plane. Within the hour, he had temporarily relocated the hub of his trust, prioritised the most urgent matters, and effectively rearranged his immediate future in anticipation of what was to come.

By the time the plane touched down on his private runway, Zak was ready and armed with every weapon he needed to ensure the outcome he wanted.

The thought that ripped through him, the one that boldly hinted that claiming his child was no guarantee that he would be a better father than his own had been, he pushed away, and rose when the plane slowed to a stop.

First he would claim his child. Then he would attempt to do what his father hadn't been able to do. Not irreparably shatter his child's life with lies and callous betrayal.

Even more determined, he headed for the master suite to wake Violet.

It was time to face this thing head on.

'Where are we?' Violet asked, blinking at the blinding sunshine pouring through the aircraft windows.

She hadn't expected to sleep for this long. Was sure she looked a sight.

The strain of delivering the news of her pregnancy and what had come afterwards had been too much to withstand. And once she'd realised there had been no way to escape

Zak, she'd barely been able to contain her composure, seeking solace in silence as a way to counteract the wild hysteria simmering just beneath the surface.

When Zak had offered the master suite, it'd been all she could do not to race from his presence and lock herself in the room as quickly as possible. Expecting to stay awake from her churning thoughts, she'd fallen into a deep sleep, the most restful she'd had since discovering she was pregnant.

Now she was awake, the enormity of the situation was even more overwhelming, not less. Aware he hadn't answered, she sucked in a breath and glanced his way.

He was waiting for her, incisive gaze devouring her as he answered, 'We're at my private island in the Caribbean.'

Of course they were.

He would hardly kidnap her and take her to a bustling metropolis where she could scream her head off and attract attention at the first opportunity, now, would he?

She shook her head. She was getting ahead of herself, fearing the worst. But how else could she explain what he done? 'You kidnapped me,' she accused, while hoping he would deny it.

He merely shrugged. 'Let's not place labels on actions just yet, shall we?'

'Of course not. Because what could be more damning than a royal prince intent on protecting his pristine image?'

His eyes narrowed on her face. 'You look better rested,' he said, smoothly changing the subject.

'In time for the interrogation you have in store for me, I'm sure.'

His sensual lips pursed and he advanced towards her, holding out his hand. 'It doesn't have to be an interrogation.'

'Oh? What do you call this, then, spiriting me thousands of miles away just to have a *discussion* with me? Did you even think to ask me or are my wishes completely irrelevant to you?'

His hand dropped like a stone, his face hardening even further. 'I told you why I was taking steps to safeguard my family's privacy. My brother just got married. My mother is weeks away from stepping down from the throne. Have you forgotten that there are those who will take advantage of another hint of scandal to further their own agendas?'

Her heart lurched, a reminder of that meeting with his defence minister rising to the fore. 'You really think they would use news of a child as a tool?' she muttered.

His hand rose again, this time more commanding. 'It's not a scenario I'm willing to wait around for or risk discovering first-hand. You will stay here until we settle things between us.'

He wasn't going to take no for an answer.

That much was evident in the watchful intensity in his eyes. But the suspicion that he wasn't giving her the full picture and that she really couldn't very well stay on the plane for ever forced her to toss aside covers she couldn't remember pulling over herself and, ignoring his outstretched hand simply because she didn't think she could withstand his touch on top of everything else, rose to her feet.

Her shoes were nowhere in sight, neither was her weekend bag.

Before she could demand their whereabouts, he reached for her, sweeping her smoothly into his arms.

She suppressed a gasp as he pressed her against his hard-muscled body, reminding her with sizzling efficiency of everything she'd tried to forget about his physical perfection. And failed. 'Put me down. I'm quite capable of walking.'

'Your things have been packed in the car, including your shoes. Unless you wish to burn your feet on the baking asphalt outside, I'm your ride.'

There was no use arguing because he was already strid-ing out of the plane.

If it hadn't been the height of absurd childishness, she would have squeezed her eyes shut and pretended he didn't exist.

But he did exist.

He was a solid unshakeable presence in her life, intent on...

What were Zak's true intentions besides the excuses he'd tossed at her? And why couldn't she stop the rush of awareness at being pressed so tightly against him?

Violet took a keener interest in her surroundings, ea-gerly wishing for anything to dissipate his effect on her. But even her surroundings were intent on assaulting her senses with an overload of beauty.

Tall palm trees swayed in the distance, a carpet of lush greenery extending left and right of the long runway as far as the eye could see. What she knew of private Caribbean islands was that they were compact, easily traversable from one end to the other.

Not this one, of course.

Several minutes after Zak had placed her in the front seat of a gleaming SUV and slid behind the wheel, they were still nowhere near their destination. Sunglasses shielded his expression from her and, apparently deciding to take a leaf from her book, he'd lapsed into silence once they were in the car.

Behind them, two more SUVs followed, one containing his bodyguards and the other with a boot full of luggage, triggering the suspicion that Zak intended to remain here for a while. It was that thought that triggered her speech.

'How long do you expect this theatre to play out?'

He slanted a glance at her. 'Theatre?'

She waved her hand at the scenery. 'You say you're try-ing to protect your family from the scandal you think my announcement will bring. But we could've had this conversation anywhere. Instead, you've brought me here to yet another symbol of your status. To what? Drive home the fact that I'm a mere commoner? You want to put me in my place, is that it?'

'Yes. All of the above,' he replied drily.

So drily, she couldn't decipher whether he was serious or joking. Then she called herself ten kinds of fool for thinking he would deny the accusation.

'I also intend to limit your access to the outside world, at least until we have a few things straightened out between us.'

'There's nothing to straighten out. I'm pregnant. I'm having a baby. End of.'

She wasn't aware of the full extent of his tension until his grip visibly relaxed on the steering wheel. 'I believe we've just settled the first thing to my satisfaction.'

About to frown, her jaw dropped as she stared at him. 'You brought me here suspecting that I wasn't going to go through with this pregnancy?'

One shoulder lifted in an eloquent shrug.

'Establishing there's a pregnancy and telling a father of his child's existence doesn't automatically mean the state is willingly accepted. Not yet, anyway.'

'What other reason could I...?' She froze, then gasped again, growing a little light-headed as his meaning sank in. 'You believe I told you about the pregnancy to leverage it? For what?'

'Off the top of my head? Everything you've ever desired since you were old enough to desire it. But your outrage is duly noted. As is your protectiveness.'

The last bit was uttered in a gruff voice, his gaze dropping to where her hand had somehow found itself over her belly again.

This time she didn't drop it or attempt to disguise the

action. They were alone, and really she was done being the soul of discretion about the child she carried. Zak had brought her here just so she'd be out of the public eye. She wasn't about to deny her child's existence.

She was still absorbing the twisted cynicism that informed his every action when they crested a low hill.

The white, sprawling plantation style house sat on top of another hill, surrounded on either side by tall swaying palm trees. And sloping away on either side, lush grass rolled away several hundred feet before turning into the white sand of a pristine beach.

All that perfection was set against a backdrop of a sparkling sea that couldn't have more stunning if it had been drawn by the world's most talented artist.

As prisons went, it was magnificent enough to snatch her breath from her lungs. On any other occasion, Violet wouldn't have stopped herself from vocalising her appreciation.

But this wasn't any other occasion. She'd been brought here for the sole purpose of being kept away from the world, a problematic stain that Prince Zakary Montegova had yet to decide what to do with.

The stony ache in her chest bruised her but she managed, barely, to hang onto her composure. She'd displayed far too many weaknesses in his presence already. The even bigger battle was ahead of her, so she had to keep her wits about her. Remain calm in the face of his highhandedness.

And find a way off this gilded paradise as soon as possible.

The moment the car drew to a stop, she reached for the door handle.

'Violet, wait—'

She ignored his growled instruction. And stepped out onto baking paving stones.

With a yelp, she sprinted towards the front door of the

mansion, fleeing the suppressed curse that sounded behind her and Zak's quick strides as he chased her down.

So much for maintaining her composure.

The doors opened smoothly and Violet skidded to a halt, her face flaming as she caught the stares of a dozen uniformed men and women who comprised the household staff.

A few glances at her attire reminded her that she was still in the gown she'd worn to Remi's wedding. Despite the air-conditioned interior, the heavy silk stuck to her skin, the short train dragging and out of place in this place where shorts and bikinis were the norm.

With her feet bare and her hair in disarray, she knew she looked a sight. Nevertheless, she plastered on a tentative smile as Zak sauntered to a stop beside her.

In deep languid tones, he made introductions, the amusement in his voice as he introduced her as Lady Violet Barringhall setting her teeth on edge.

There was nothing ladylike about her appearance. And it was all his fault. Once the majority of the staff had dispersed, they were left with the head butler.

'We'll take refreshments in the living room, Patrick,' Zak said, and then he caught hold of her wrist.

Violet went along with him simply because she didn't want to give an even worse impression of herself in front of his staff. The moment they were alone, she wrenched herself from his grasp.

'We can finish this thing now. I'm sure it'll only take a few minutes. Then you can get me off this island.'

He waved a hand at one exquisite striped sofa. 'Sit down, Violet.'

'I'm getting tired of you ordering me about, Zak.'

'You're a guest in my house and I'm offering you due courtesy.'

'I'm not a guest. I'm your prisoner. Let's get at least one thing straight.'

His face tightened. 'Very well. If you think yourself a prisoner then you should be aware of a few things. There is no way off the island except by boat or air, both of which are under my strict command. Attempt to solicit help from the staff and you will merely be embarrassing yourself. Is that clear?'

She swallowed a knot of disappointment.

He raised an eyebrow. 'Did I just shatter your dreams?'

She forced a laugh. 'Don't flatter yourself.'

For a second, a bewildered look chased across his face but it was extinguished just as quickly. 'Would you like a tour of the property? Most people are content with being in the lap of luxury. Perhaps you'll change your mind after you've seen the place properly?'

'If you wanted me to view this place as anything but a prison, you should've tried inviting me instead of kidnapping me.'

'Would you have come?'

The question was so unexpected it left her speechless for a moment. Would she have dropped everything to spend time with Zak on his island paradise? When self-preservation alone dictated that she stay as far away from him as possible? 'No.'

His nostrils flared briefly. 'Then I have my answer.'

'For someone so hell-bent on safeguarding your family's reputation, don't you think this is merely compounding it? What's to stop me from going straight to the tabloids and reporting you to the authorities once you set me free? Or do you intend to keep me here for ever?'

'Now, there's a thought,' he drawled.

The notion that he would even consider such a thing had her stalking over to where he lounged in the chair, master and commander of all he surveyed. 'This isn't funny, Zak.'

'I'm most definitely not laughing. Sit down, Violet,' he invited silkily, but with an edge to his voice that sent a shiver over her skin.

Because close proximity to Zak was a bad idea, and because she needed to gain some much-needed solid ground, she retreated to the farthest seat from him and sat down just as the butler entered, bearing a tray of drinks.

She accepted a glass of fruit punch, only realising how thirsty she was after the first sip. She set the glass down with a resolute click. 'How long do you intend to keep me here?'

'That depends.'

'On what?'

'On how agreeable you are to my terms.'

'What terms?'

Dark grey eyes locked on hers.

'No child, besides Jules, has been born out of wedlock in Montegovan royal history. And I'm sure you know the circumstances surrounding how my half-brother arrived in my family.'

'I only know what I read in the tabloids. So unless you're claiming those allegations weren't true?'

'For the most part, *si*, they were true,' he stated tightly, his voice discouraging further interest.

It was clear this was a subject Zak didn't like discussing. 'Okay, but what does that have to do with the child I'm carrying?'

He regarded her with unwavering intent. 'What do you think, Violet?'

Suspecting what was coming, she reeled in disbelief and shock. 'Whatever it is, the answer is no.'

One eyebrow lifted. 'I haven't even asked you yet.'

'No,' she repeated.

'Yes, Violet. I bear responsibility for the lack of protection when we had sex, but you also assured me that there was no risk of pregnancy. But what's done is done. While I'm curious to know why your contraception failed, it's immaterial at this point. You're carrying my child and I intend to claim it.'

A handful of words with consequences that stretched far into her future. She folded her hands tightly in her lap to disguise their trembling. 'What exactly does that mean?'

'It means my child will bear my name, be brought up in Montegova under my care, take pride in his or her heritage, be afforded every privilege and welcome the responsibilities every royal Montegovan is due. And all of that will come about if his birth comes with the benefit of true legitimacy. Which is why the only sensible recourse is for you to marry me.'

Contrary to the near hysteria that had threatened to overwhelm her mere moments ago, an eerie sense of calm settled over Violet once he'd said the actual words.

'No,' she stated once again, thrilled when her voice emerged firm and solid.

Shock flashed crossed his face. Then his eyes narrowed. 'No? That's all you have to say? No?'

'Pardon me, where are my manners? No, *thank you*,' she amended, secretly thrilled when he immediately looked… perturbed again.

'Perhaps you didn't hear me properly. I want you to marry me, Violet. You will have the title of Princess, wealth beyond your wildest imagination, and, if you wish it a place in my trust to continue your career.'

Marry me.

Her heart lurched as those two words, contrary to everything she'd believed of herself and her future path, making her waver for a moment as she was inundated with might-have-beens. Her fingers bunched tighter. 'I heard you, loud and clear. And you heard my answer.'

For a full minute Zak stared at her, his gaze unashamedly probing, seeming to delve beneath her skin. Then he eased back in his seat, his face turning alarmingly neutral.

She wasn't fooled for a second by the arm he raised to rest on the back of his sofa, or the legs he casually crossed.

'It's been an…unsettling twenty-four hours. Perhaps you would like some time to consider all this?' he suggested.

She summoned a small, hopefully dismissive smile. 'What, the fragile little lady needs some time to wrap her head around everything that's happening to her? Isn't that just typical of your sort?'

One eyebrow elevated. And was that a tic going in his jaw? 'My sort?'

'Half-decent-looking men of means who believe all they need to do is crook their finger at a woman to have her swooning at their feet.'

'Since I have first-hand evidence that you've never been intimately acquainted with any other man, even my sort, I'll assume this is a sweeping generalisation?'

Her pretended calm threatened to evaporate as a warm flush consumed her face. Still, she managed a shrug. 'Are you sure you can trust this evidence? For all you know, I could've been living it up in New York while you were… wherever you decided to swan off to.'

The tic intensified and the look he sent her was anything but neutral. It thrummed with volcanic fury. 'I was in Australia. And for your sake, I hope you're merely attempting to get a rise out of me.'

'What if I am? Will that earn me a quick exit off this island?' she countered.

His face tightened and she could've sworn his stomach muscles clenched hard. 'It won't, but confirmation of a dalliance with another man while you carry my child will definitely not sit well. Did you?' he enquired with smooth, silky lethality.

Violet held his gaze in bold silence for a handful of seconds before the denial erupted from her throat. 'No, I didn't. But I assure you, I won't be a well-behaved little prisoner if you insist on keeping me here. In fact, I'm certain you will regret it if you don't put me back on that plane immediately.'

A layer of that ferocious tension eased from his frame as he took a slow, controlled breath, that regal head cocked mockingly. 'We have time. Please, enlighten me as to how you plan to make my life difficult.'

And allow him to use that shrewd steel trap of a mind to counter her strategy? Not likely. 'Don't worry, you'll find out soon enough if you insist on pursuing this absurd caper. And it's not just me you'll have to contend with, you know. Did you stop to think about how my mother would take my disappearance at all? Do you think she's going to just sit by and allow you to kidnap her daughter?'

Without the slightest hint of unease, he shrugged. 'I'm confident I can handle your mother. Next.'

Unfortunately, Violet believed him. She suspected he could have her mother eating out of his hand with minimum effort.

Her heart clenched with that shame she'd never managed to shrug off when it came to her mother's blatantly grasping antics. Heck, she was fairly certain Zak would receive a resounding endorsement of this kidnapping from her mother if it meant she could brag about it ad nauseam at future dinner parties.

As for the discovery that Violet was pregnant, it was why she'd guarded her new state with feverish zeal. Why she intended to keep it under wraps for as long as possible. Her mother's discovery that she carried the next Montego-van royal would see her thrust into the sort of limelight her mother adored but Violet desperately abhorred.

Nevertheless, she couldn't keep this a secret for ever. Neither could she avoid her mother for ever.

And it certainly didn't mean she wanted to be kept here against her will, regardless of how stunning this prison was. She pursed her lips. 'How about your staff? You employ the type of people who condone kidnapping, do you?' she taunted.

'Their loyalty is absolute and faultless or they wouldn't be here,' he stated, his voice deep, firm and completely unfazed by her cold accusations.

About to challenge him some more, she froze for a moment, unsure why until the distant rumble of aircraft engines had her surging to her feet. She rushed to the French doors in time to see the jet rising gracefully into the sky, its wings glinting in the dappling sunlight.

'No!' She whirled towards him, fury and an emotion she refused to name flaming through her veins at the realisation that she was alone, secluded and stranded, on an island with Zak Montegova.

'Yes,' he countered smoothly. 'Calm down, Violet.'

'No, I won't calm down. You want another reason? How about the simple fact that I don't want this? That what you're doing is plain wrong?'

He simply shrugged, unfazed by her outburst. 'As you can see, it's going to take more than the seductive promise of a temper tantrum to change my mind about this.' His voice was low, deep, sexy in an authoritative way that highlighted his innate masculinity.

A shiver danced through her.

Seductive? Did Zak actually want her to throw a tantrum? Recalling that their last two arguments had ended up with varying degrees of intimacy, the second achieving the ultimate, she fought a blush and decided then and there to do the exact opposite.

She was paying the ultimate price for her folly in Tanzania. There was no need to throw more fuel on a fire that had almost consumed her once already.

And how could she have forgotten that mere hours after the fact he'd done a disappearing act on her? That he wouldn't be taking this course of action if he didn't have a selfish reason in mind.

By flailing and protesting at every turn, was she playing right into his hands? Several scenarios tumbled through her mind, each one as disturbing as the last. She slowly sucked in a calm breath, ignoring her thundering heart.

After one last longing look at the aircraft, which was now a tiny speck in the sky, she turned back to him. 'Very well. You want to play this game? Don't say I didn't warn you.'

The raw glint that lit his eyes for a few stomach-hollowing seconds sent a wave of panic through her. It reeked of relished anticipation. Of the kind of marauding conquests his ancestors were renowned for and Montegovans were intensely proud of. He didn't exactly say the words, *bring it on*, but they flamed in his eyes for those seconds before Zak rose, all litheness, power and blood-quickening animalistic grace, to stride assuredly to where she stood. And up close, she saw something else.

Sexual attraction.

He may have avoided her for weeks after Tanzania, may have pretended she didn't exist at his brother's wedding. But Zak still desired her.

And, damn her, her body's wild and fierce surging to life announced that the feeling was intensely mutual. But feeling was one thing. Acting on those feelings quite another. She intended to deny every ounce of this fevered attraction if it was the last thing she did. She'd already spent far too many nights dwelling on why she couldn't get this man out of her damned head.

'Now that we've established you're staying for the foreseeable future, would you like to familiarise yourself with the property?' he asked, all arrogant charm and effortless masculinity.

About to snap that she wasn't in the mood to tour her prison, she swallowed the heated words.

Self-containment.

Aloofness.

Grace.

She would epitomise the very word if it killed her. 'Maybe later. I'm rather tired. Just point me in the direction of where I'm to sleep and I'll get out of your hair.'

Wary suspicion narrowed his eyes. She would've laughed if she wasn't terrified he would see through her intentions, somehow find a way to dismantle them. Hadn't he done that very thing by that waterfall in Tanzania?

After an interminable minute, he gave a curt nod. He curled his fingers around her wrist and Violet fought a wild, frenzied battle not to pull away. That would be admitting his touch seared her deep, awakening sensations she was absolutely loath to admit she'd missed—even craved—in the weeks of his absence.

Nevertheless, she didn't intend to allow him such careless courtesies. So, under the pretext of returning to her seat to retrieve her clutch, she smoothly eased her hand from his.

The merest flaring of his nostrils was the only indication that he'd noticed. Making sure to keep a few necessary feet between them, she walked with him to the door.

Together they climbed a wide, sweeping staircase, at the top of which were hallways that branched out in two directions. Zak took the east hallway, leading her to the farthest set of doors.

He threw them open and Violet barely suppressed a gasp. The suite was tasteful magnificence personified. A different level of luxury from the rooms at the Montegovan palace but jaw-dropping nonetheless. Eggshell-blue walls and white muslin curtains gave the room a light and airy feel.

Cleverly accented with pale gold fixtures and furnishings, she felt as if she was floating in the sunlit sky.

The grounding force in the form of the solid, powerful man who was watching her with a steady gaze brought her back down to earth.

'A tray of refreshments will be brought up to you. We will have dinner at seven. If you need me before then, the staff will tell you where to find me.'

'Why on earth would I need you?'

A mocking smile twitched the corner of his sensual lips. 'To give me your answer, of course.'

In all the furore surrounding her kidnap, she'd momentarily forgotten that he'd asked her, *no, decreed* that she marry him.

A pulse of shock ricocheted through her. She curbed a hysterical snort. If anyone had told her just yesterday that Zak would demand that she wed him, and that she would actually *forget* that demand, she'd have crowed with laughter.

She raised a hand to her head as it threatened to spin. Instantly, he was before her, cupping her shoulders in a firm hold and frowning down at her. 'What's wrong?' he asked tersely.

'I'm just…a little dizzy.' And the warm, seductive fire of his touch wasn't helping.

His lips flattened. 'You've worn yourself out.'

'No, *you've* worn me out. Leave, please. I really want to be alone.'

He didn't release her. As he'd done when they'd left the plane, he swung her up into his arms, strode a few steps to where the huge, queen-size bed, festooned with pillows, waited. With a gentleness belying the bristling purpose stamped on his face, he set her down in the middle of it, slid the cover from beneath her and, with one sizzling scrutiny from head to toe, settled it back over her.

'I'd offer to help remove that dress, but I'm guessing you're going to oppose me on principle,' he drawled.

'Give the Prince a prize,' she responded drily.

For a moment he froze, his eyes narrowing ominously. She held her breath, a curiously hot and heavy anticipation oozing through her belly.

Then, instead of the sharp retort she'd expected, he extended his hand, trailed his forefinger down one cheek in a silent, electrifying caress.

Violet was glad the covers hid her body's reaction. And while she was battling the pearling of her nipples and the damp neediness between her thighs, he stepped back.

'Rest now. We will pick this up again later.'

She chose silence. Because all of a sudden she wasn't sure she wanted him to leave. Actually felt curiously bereft in the pit of her stomach as his broad-shouldered frame headed for the door.

And when she winced at the gentle but definitive snick of the door shutting, she feared how deflated she felt, as if he'd taken her very vitality with him. As if he'd dimmed the sun with his absence.

More than anything that'd happened since she'd stepped onto the plane what felt like a lifetime ago, it was what terrified her the most.

CHAPTER EIGHT

SHE WAS STILL choosing silence two weeks later.

A fact, she was very pleased to note, that had increasingly aggravated the hitherto unflappable Prince Zak Montegova. He didn't overtly display his displeasure at her attitude, but it was there in the flattening of his sensual lips when she left the table immediately after a civil but silent meal.

In the brisk stride of his departure when her monosyllabic answers stifled his attempt at conversation.

In her ability to project an outwardly cool and dismissive demeanour when she caught him staring at her with blatant heat in his eyes, while every cell in her body thrilled to that electric look.

In the flaring of his nostrils when he asked, 'Are you ready to give me your answer?'

And was met with an even-toned, 'Yes. It's still no.'

For the most part Violet congratulated herself on maintaining a decent enough composure. The only moments of vulnerability happened six days into her enforced stay, when she woke to hear the sound of a different sort of engine. The sleek speedboat had delivered a distinguished-looking Montegovan doctor and his two assistants, and myriad quantity of medical equipment, including a state-of-the-art portable ultrasound machine.

She hid her joy, unwilling to show Zak how much she'd been yearning to hear her baby's heartbeat for the first time.

He threatened to ruin the moment when, watching the equipment being set up, he leaned low to rasp in her ear,

'If you're thinking of spilling your guts to the doctor or his team, don't bother. He's been my personal physician since birth. I trust him implicitly. But should he even consider being disloyal, trust that I have far more extensive resources to secure his discretion than you could ever dream up.'

She hated herself for her sharp, vulnerable intake of breath. For the arrow of hurt that lodged in her midriff. More than anything, she hated herself for having considered doing exactly that, then instantly dismissing it with no clear reason why she'd abandon such an expedient route off the island. 'You're a bastard, do you know that?' she hissed.

His face hardened as he stared down at her. 'I'm a lot of things, *mia carina*, but that label isn't one of them. It's also a label I wish to prevent my child from wearing, if only you'd see sense,' he sliced at her, the edge in his voice momentarily setting hers aflame.

That she was absurdly glad for that glimpse of a deeper reaction from him only intensified when, stretched out in her bed minutes later, she watched the monitor in awe as she looked at the grainy picture of her child, and then redirected her gaze to Zak at his unfettered intake of breath.

His raw, naked expression, his inability to look away from the monitor or his complete unawareness that he'd grasped her hand, wrapped dangerously tender strings around her chest. She clung to him, aware that her guard had disintegrated, that she yearned to ask him how he truly felt about the baby she was carrying.

'Everything is precisely as it should be,' the doctor announced then, shattering the moment. 'Congratulations, Your Highness.' He turned to her, his professionalism not quite hiding the speculation in his eyes. 'And to you, Lady Barringhall.'

Zak started, his stormy gaze dropping down to hers. The next instant, he'd reclaimed his composure, directing a dark frown at their entwined hands before calmly disengaging his. Then, arms stiffly folded, he proceeded to direct questions at his doctor.

Despite his withdrawal, Violet hadn't been able to quite catch her breath, the notion that Zak might feel something deeper for his child other than as his heir threatening her composure.

Made her pause for a millisecond to consider…possibilities. Rationally, she knew his imperiously worded proposal was because of the child she carried. That he intended to wrap the tight cloak of royalty and privilege and years of history around his child.

But was there something more?

And what about her?

If she'd learned anything from her mother's feverish ambitions to marry her daughters off to rich, titled husbands for her own selfish ends, it was that those kinds of marriages were shockingly common. And, more often than not, it left one or both participants jaded and miserable within a few years, resulting in infidelity or the kind of open marriages whispered about at dinner parties.

The very thing she'd striven for years to get away from.

But had this gone beyond *her*?

Was she holding out for what she wanted in complete disregard for the needs of her child? Would her baby despise her one day for the choices she'd made? For choosing her own path instead of bowing down to the decree of its father?

Was she allowing her own childhood experiences to cloud her judgement to the detriment of her unborn child? But wasn't that what parents were supposed to do? Carefully weigh options and decide what was best for their child?

Was that what Zak had been doing? It occurred to her then that everything she knew about Zak had been mostly second-hand.

Except for that kiss.

Except for that unforgettable episode in Tanzania.

But that was just sex. She didn't actually know the man. And…some of that blame lay with her. Didn't it?

Do you even know anything about his childhood?

She pushed the thought away, the notion that she was beginning to make excuses for her chilly silence these past two weeks eating at her.

He'd kidnapped her.

Yes, but it hadn't turned out to be the nightmare she'd envisaged, had it? While she'd refused to explore the island on principle, she'd availed herself of the extensive library adjoining Zak's study, been secretly thrilled to discover a wealth of conservation books she'd been dying to read.

Not to mention the personal treats he'd showered on her.

For the first week, a new delivery had arrived by boat every day, starting with two dozen boxes stuffed with designer wear perfect for idling about on a tropical island. Light, airy sundresses, tasteful bikinis and sandals, sunglasses and wide-brimmed hats in every shade. No detail had been left unsatisfied.

Then came the daily delivery of flowers, each time with a different gift.

A diamond tennis bracelet. A large basket of cashmere knitting yarn following her brief conversation with the housekeeper about wanting to pick up the hobby. Expensive exquisitely scented candles specially crafted for expectant mothers. A pen drive containing a drone's-eye view of the completed project in Tanzania.

But best of the lot had been the small, framed photo of the ultrasound image of her baby. A photo she kept propped up on her bedside and the first thing she saw each morning.

It was that gesture that had triggered her questioning the unshakeable *no* she'd delivered every time Zak had asked her to marry him. Or perhaps it was more the fact that he hadn't asked in the last three days?

She massaged mildly throbbing temples. Was she suffering some weird form of Stockholm syndrome? Softening just when she needed to harden her heart against her captor?

She looked around her now, at the sparkling pool and the pristine beach beyond. At the stunning beauty all around her. It didn't look or feel like a prison. The staff were friendly and courteous with her, treated Zak with a respect and reverence that went beyond employee/prince boundaries.

Impatient with her thoughts and unable to concentrate on the book she was reading, she rose from the sun lounger that had become her outdoor refuge. She would've stayed in her room the whole time had it not signalled weakness. Instead, she'd flaunted her calm indifference in his face, let him taste her triumph, the way she had when he'd walked in on her opening the clothing boxes after their arrival.

He'd studied her with those piercing eyes, probably expecting her to gush her gratitude or throw a tantrum at her incarceration. Instead she'd calmly thanked him, instructed the staff to deposit the clothes in her dressing room, then, after sliding into the most provocative bikini she could find, she'd returned downstairs.

She knew she'd succeeded in scoring a point when he'd inhaled sharply at her appearance in the library with a shockingly large surface area of her body on display. Ignoring him, she'd sashayed to the extensive bookcase, taken her time to select a psychological thriller, then made her exit, head held high.

So why was she faltering now?

Because this stand-off couldn't continue for ever.

Her mother's emails were getting more frequent and strident and she wasn't being mollified by Violet's evasive replies. It was only a matter of time before Margot connected the dots and did something foolish. Like pick up the phone to her favourite tabloid magazine to voice her concern for her daughter's whereabouts.

With a sigh, she turned away from the breathtaking view, her mind whirling as she entered the living room.

And came face to face with Zak.

They stared at each other. No, it was more than that. They *absorbed* each other. The air thickened with a heavy, crackling awareness, churning displeasure and...*sex* in a volatile mix that quickened her heartbeat.

Or was it the vitality and pure, raw masculinity that brimmed from him, the mouth she couldn't stop thinking about kissing even as she remained steeped in her role of indifference, and the blinding white linen lounge clothes he'd taken to wearing on the island that was severely wrecking her equilibrium?

Whatever it was, it locked her in place. Until her lungs burned, and her senses screamed for self-preservation.

They snapped into motion at the same time, Zak heading for her with ferocious determination etched into his face. She attempted to bypass him by skirting the sofa. And failed when he cornered her a few feet from the door, his towering body barring her way.

'Excuse me,' she said, cringing when her customary coolness emerged hot and husky.

'No, *cara*, you're not excused.'

He blocked her escape by the simple act of placing his hands on the exquisite Venetian-papered wall on either side of her, caging her in, making her shockingly aware of how much of her skin was exposed in the orange bikini and the matching sarong that only covered her hips and upper thighs.

'What are you—?'

'Enough of this, Violet,' he breathed, his voice a dangerous volcanic rumble that merely heightened her sensual awareness of him. 'It's been two weeks.'

In a wild bid to reverse the frantic beat of her heart at his proximity, she took her time to slot her bookmark between the pages of her novel before tossing it on a console table nearby. Only then did she gather every shred of composure to meet his eyes. 'If it's too much for you, you know what you need to do to end it.'

For a long stretch he didn't answer, the only sound in the room the lazy whirling of the ceiling fan. And her agitated breathing.

His gaze raked her body before returning to rest on her face. 'You intend to go on letting us both suffer in silence?'

'Which one bothers you more, the suffering or the silence?' she asked, noting again how her voice missed the flippancy she'd aimed for.

An arrogant, sexy smile draped his lips, even while his eyes remained shrewd, watchful. Calculating. 'You wish me to bare myself so you can subject me to even more of the same treatment?'

Her smile was saccharine sweet. 'If you would be so kind.'

The smile evaporated. Her skin tingled and her senses jumped as rigid purpose tightened his features. He leaned forward until his lips were a scant inch from her ear. 'Did you not learn your lesson about crossing swords with me in Tanzania, Violet?' he murmured softly, dangerously in her ear.

She couldn't stop the shiver that racked her frame. She angled herself away from him, aware she was in danger of disgracing herself by toppling over but not caring in that moment. 'Are you threatening me?' Why did the very thought make her senses shiver in anticipation, make the flesh between her legs swell with need?

'I'm threatening you with the exact reaction you've been hoping for since embarking on this…escapade.'

* * *

Just like in Tanzania, just like in every interaction he'd ever had with this breathtaking creature, Zak felt unnerved, unbalanced. For as long as he could remember, every moment of his life had been shaped in strict conformity, that secret yearning to be an exemplary son to a seemingly exemplary father directing him to life in the military. While he'd had his share of liaisons, they'd been discreet, with no incidence of drama that might bring embarrassment to him or his family.

His father had not only betrayed *him* and everything Zak had believed was an honourable legacy, he'd plunged his entire family into scandal and endangered Montegova. That time was seared onto his psyche, had driven him to be extremely circumspect in his own relationships. He staunchly believed his immunity to soft words and lofty promises granted him a gratifying insight into people's true characters. He'd learned never to accept anyone at face value. Never to fall into seductive traps.

So far, his only stumbling blocks had been an unforgettable kiss six years ago, a moment of insanity at a stunning waterfall, and a ruthless decision to kidnap.

All incidents that involved Violet.

The unsettling part of it all was…he wouldn't change a single thing.

With each passing day, he wanted the child in her womb with a deeper fervour. Blood of his blood. Flesh of his flesh. Under his care.

A chance to rewrite history?

Perhaps it was a little selfish, but what if he achieved the impossible and got right what his father had got so wrong? What if he engendered loyalty, trust, integrity…even affection in his child, traits he'd believed were a cornerstone of his own life until he'd discovered otherwise. What if he could help his heir…thrive?

Wasn't that worth pursuing this course of action with Violet? Wasn't it worth living temporarily with this hollow pit in his stomach that whispered that he could fail?

He wouldn't, of course. He *couldn't*. This was too... vital. But he did admit things hadn't turned out the way he'd envisaged.

For starters, he'd expected her to throw a tantrum. Perhaps even pout and plead while she pretended to play hard to get over his proposal. Right before she fell into line with his wishes.

Instead she'd treated him with cool, sustained, never-ending *indifference*.

It *grated*. He was used to women falling over themselves to gain his attention. Had experienced it at a near nauseating level at Remi's wedding when, with his brother newly off the market, even more avid eyes had turned his way.

On that occasion, he'd withstood their interest simply to avoid the temptation to stare at and fill his senses again with Violet at every opportunity.

Now he wanted an *engagement* of a specific sort. The kind that gave him free rein to touch her glowing skin, to attract a smile that didn't start and end with mild disdain.

To have her not deliver that vacant smile when their paths crossed, then look through him as if he wasn't there. The first few days he'd been amused. Then he'd been irritated.

Then a dismaying feeling had overwhelmed him that she was getting steeped in this role she'd determinedly taken to freeze him out. It was that feeling ballooning out of proportion that'd ejected him from his study in the middle of a workday, his concentration a shambles of shattered focus and intense vexation. The sensation of losing time and ground with Violet had demanded he seek her out, finally end this nonsense.

Of course, the impact of her smooth golden skin, long-legged grace and those blue eyes had seemed more vivid each time he looked into them had all played a part, too, wreaking carnage with his body.

So…one way or the other, the cold, silent treatment was ending now. Before he lost his mind.

One side effect of pregnancy she'd dreaded was morning sickness. Another one Violet hadn't quite anticipated was a heightened sense of smell.

The moment she inhaled Zak's unique masculine scent, her senses went into overdrive. Heat fired up in her pelvis, the blood rushed into her breasts, hardening her nipples as fine tremors invaded her body.

In desperation, she licked her lips. His eyes darkened as he followed the swipe of her tongue, his chest expanding on a deep breath.

'We'll need to discuss this rationally sooner or later—'

'Why do you want to saddle yourself with me, Zak?' she blurted, her earlier misgivings furiously resurfacing. 'You don't even know me. Not really. And I don't know you, save for what's bandied about on the internet. I could be your worst nightmare. Let me go and in a few months' time we can discuss shared custody—'

'No.' A blaze of possessiveness in his eyes accompanied the hard refusal.

'You won't even—'

'Let's change things a little,' he said smoothly, intent eyes riveted on the pulse leaping at her throat.

'What?'

'Let's call a temporary truce to all this nonsense. You say I don't know you. So show me the real Violet Barringhall underneath all this stiff upper lip thing that I assure you has got quite tedious.'

The offer tantalised and tempted. But it felt one-sided,

especially in the light of her own thoughts about him only minutes ago. 'What do I get in return?'

'Reciprocity.' Before her senses could jump in wild giddiness at the offer, he added, 'Up to a point.'

Disappointment bit deep. 'You're already ring-fencing your offer?'

An inscrutable veil descended over his face. 'I'm not in the habit of offering myself up *carte blanche* to anyone. I'm not going to start now.'

Disappointment turned to hurt. Why was she surprised? She was just another being beneath his regard, one who just happened to be carrying his child.

But since it was clear Zak intended to claim this child in one way or another, wasn't she better off knowing the man better? Knowledge was power, wasn't it?

About to grudgingly accept his offer of a truce, she snatched in a breath as another scent pervaded her nostrils. Geraldine, the housekeeper, was probably preparing another delectable snack. But not one Violet's senses appreciated. She felt her stomach fold in on itself as nausea rose, harsh and fast.

The frantic need to make it to the bathroom, to not disgrace herself, had her ducking beneath his arm.

'Violet?' Zak reached for her, concern etched into his face.

She shook her head, fleeing towards one of the endless bathrooms in the villa. She barely made it before emptying the contents of her stomach into the bowl.

Over and over her insides surged as the mild morning sickness she'd experienced only once three days ago and had foolishly believed had permanently disappeared returned with a vengeance.

She'd dislodged her hat during her mad dash, and now she felt strong, gentle hands gather her hair in a loose hold, away from the trajectory of her humiliation. Squeezing her eyes shut, she willed the nausea down, grasping for a modicum of self-respect. Just as another bout hit her hard.

'Easy, *carina*,' Zak crooned in a deep, low voice, one hand sweeping down her back in a gentle caress.

Spent and breathless, she laughed. Or at least attempted to. 'There's nothing easy about morning sickness. It's horrible and humiliating and…' She stopped, closed her eyes as tears threatened to compound her misery.

'*Si*, I get the picture.'

Opening her eyes, she glared at him. 'And you standing there, looking like the spokesperson for health and vitality isn't helping, trust me.'

'I shall locate my sackcloth forthwith,' he said with deep solemnity.

Against all sense of self-preservation, her lips curved in a small smile. 'This isn't funny.'

'No,' he agreed.

'Stop trying to humour me.'

Again he nodded. 'How can I help, Violet?'

Utterly disarmed by the offer, she stared nonplussed for several seconds before reason kicked in. All this was for his child's benefit. Nothing more. 'You can go away.'

'No. I believe you were about to accept my offer of a truce before this unfortunate incident. Let's not ruin the progress we were making.' The words slid smoothly from his lips, one hand held out to her while the other flushed the toilet.

Perhaps she was weak. Perhaps she was tired of this chilly standoff that had achieved nothing but a stalemate and fleeting satisfaction at childish needling.

Before she could stop herself, Violet slid her hand into his. He helped her up and led her to the marble-topped sink. From the discreet little vanity, he took out a bottle of mouthwash, poured a measure in a glass and handed it to her.

'Thank you.'

While she rinsed her mouth, and welcomed the minty taste that replaced the vileness, he ran a towel under cool water and dabbed it against her temples.

It felt heavenly, so soothing she couldn't hold back a moan.

Zak froze, his eyes dark and ravenous as he stared down at her. Her breath caught, her temperature ramping up at the blatantly carnal gaze he didn't bother to disguise. His hand continued its gentle ministrations, over her cheeks, her jaw, down to the wild tattoo beating at her throat.

He noted the helpless little shiver that went through her, tossed the towel into the sink, then moved purposefully between her knees. Still pinning her with his potent gaze, he slid his fingers into her hair, angled her face up to his.

'Wh-what are you doing?'

'We're having a moment, Violet. Just let it be,' he rasped.

A deep yearning to do exactly as he wished saturated her veins. But all he did was run his thumb over her lower lip, seemingly content to just caress her, while she craved more. So much more than was wise.

Sharp disappointment lanced her when he stepped back and released her.

His gaze remained latched on her mouth for another spell before his eyes rose to hers. 'The truce, Violet. Will you accept it?' he pressed.

The thought of returning to cold detachment didn't appeal. She didn't intend to turn warm and fuzzy, she remained his captive after all. But... 'Yes. But with a stipulation of my own.'

He tensed. *'Si?'*

'Three days. That's all I'll give you.'

Determination blazed in his eyes. 'One week.'

She rolled hers. 'Fine. One week. After that I'm getting off this island, even if I have to swim.'

One brow mockingly cocked. 'Is that so?'

'*Si,*' she mimicked him. 'That, or I go back to driving you crazy.'

His nostrils flared and something curiously close to relish lit his eyes before he veiled his expression. 'Agreed.'

It felt far too easy but with his iron-willed control back in place, she couldn't read him. Especially not when he held out his hand again.

'Despite your stubborn refusal to stray beyond the swimming pool, you must be dying to see the rest of the island.'

She was. Especially the green hills teeming with vegetation that bordered the north side of the island. She looked down at herself. 'Do I need to change?'

His hot gaze raked her, leaving every exposed inch of her skin hyperaware and sensitive. 'You're fine as you are. Come.'

Not even the imperious command eroded her excitement as they left the villa and headed for the fleet of sleek custom-made golf buggies she'd seen the staff use. Zak chose the most pristine one, a six-seater complete with air-conditioning and drinks cabinet.

After seeing her seated, he slid behind the wheel. Violet averted her gaze from his strong, muscled thighs and the brawny forearms. She knew the chaos that body could wreak on hers.

Despite having her world reduced to several thousand square feet for the last two weeks, albeit in unspeakable luxury, she experienced a trace of apprehension as they left the villa behind.

Realising she was in danger of growing attached to her prison or, even worse, falling in love with Zak's villa, she stopped herself from looking back, concentrating on the swaying palm trees that gradually gave way to denser vegetation and steeper hills.

'How big is this place?' she asked, desperate to dilute

the sensually charged atmosphere and Zak's unapologetic gaze that raked over her every few minutes.

If she'd devised a way to drive him to the edge by her indifference, he'd found a much more effective way of returning the favour with his blatant scrutiny.

'Altogether, it's over three thousand square acres. There are three separate beaches and a natural diving platform, among several interesting things.'

Those interesting things left her awed and dumbstruck.

The island was ninety per cent self-sufficient. A small desalination and water purification plant recycled sea-and rainwater for the island, solar panels provided electricity and an unobtrusive water irrigation system served a farm that reared a handful of Wagyu beef cattle, free-range chickens and provided an extensive selection of vegetables.

Despite the size of the island, it turned out that less than a quarter of the acreage had been developed, leaving the rest as a nature preserve with a dozen tastefully blended eco-lodges for the super-wealthy who wished to enhance their awareness of conservation.

Violet didn't want to be impressed but she couldn't quite hide her stunned awe. Neither could she dismiss the troubling revelation that under normal circumstances she would've enjoyed spending time exploring the island. Even…stayed of her own free will.

The wide-scale alarm she'd expected at the thought never arrived.

God, what was wrong with her? Was she softening? Falling in love with her prison? Pardoning Zak when she should be fighting him every step of the way?

'What were you doing in Australia?' she asked, desperate to dredge up her outrage, remind herself that he couldn't get away from her fast enough after Tanzania.

Zak turned away from the bluff at the highest point of the island where they'd stopped to enjoy the breathtaking view. His shrug bore no hint of regret. 'That part of the world suffers the same humanitarian challenges.'

'Did you leave to avoid me?' she pressed. The question was infinitely presumptuous but she didn't take it back. She needed to know. Despite her thumping heart. Despite the hurt that would accompany his confirmation.

He stiffened, his eyes narrowing on her face. 'Are we dropping our civility already, Violet?'

'You think it's uncivil to ask for the truth?'

'Not at all. But are you prepared for the answer?'

She bit the inside of her cheek, suddenly afraid of his answer. But wasn't this a laying-yourself-bare exercise, at least on her part, so she would truly know the type of man she was dealing with?

She swallowed, boldly met his gaze. 'Yes.'

His jaw tensed. Silence stretched, the wind ruffling his thick hair drawing her gaze to the perfection of his face. When he stepped closer, she gasped at the raw, carnal look in his eyes. 'You're not unaware of your beauty, Violet. I left because I didn't trust my ability to stick to what we'd agreed.'

'Wh-what are you saying?'

He reached for a strand of hair, tossed against her cheek by the breeze. For another short stretch he caressed the silky tendril. Then he pierced her with his gaze. 'That I would've wanted you in my bed, repeatedly, if I'd stayed in New York,' he stated baldly.

Her breath strangled to nothing, her body screaming awake at the imagery his words evoked. 'Zak…'

'I had to go to the other side of the world to get this… need under control.'

'Was that all?' The idea that there could be another reason, perhaps the same one that'd made him walk away from her that night six years ago, burned deep and painful. 'I'm only asking because, despite this little confession, you barely acknowledged me at your brother's wedding,' she said, hating herself for the lash of jealousy and irritation the reminder brought.

Or was she fooling herself? Was it just bruised pride? Or something more precious?

She pushed the thought away as he laughed. 'You believe you're that easily forgettable?' With the growled words, he reached for her, driving his fingers into her hair.

Unlike the charged coming together that had fuelled their past intimate encounters, this was a slow burn of a kiss. But it was no less earth-shattering or all-consuming. Perhaps even more so because the sensations coursing through her body were even more frightening, a clamour that scared her with its sheer depth.

The sweep of his tongue over her lips, the tightening of his hold, and the scent of him all converged to fire up a need so strong she didn't question the wisdom of sliding her hands around his trim waist, digging her fingers into the small of his back and, with another deep moan, straining upward to deepen the kiss.

One hand left her hair to glide down her back, his touch more urgent, more insistent as he dragged her closer. Her sensitive breasts flattened against his chest, his hard body a hot, living column branding her.

She opened for him, their tongues dancing an erotic tango, driving every thought from her head save the need to perpetuate this heady encounter.

'*Dio mio*, but you intoxicate me,' he muttered against her lips.

And he more than intoxicated her. He made her *need*. Made her crave the impossible.

Their breaths mingled, sharing the same air as he deepened the kiss.

When the need for more oxygen drove them apart, hot slashes of colour heating his chiselled cheekbones. Against her belly, he was as hard as steel and it fired up that hot and needy space between her legs.

'Does this feel under control to you, Violet?' he breathed. 'I've watched you parade around with your haughty little nose in the air and your sinful body on display, and I can barely think straight for wanting you beneath me.'

There was nowhere to hide. Her nipples puckered, her lips parting on a desperate intake of breath as she struggled to contain the fire raging through her.

He tucked her hair over one ear. 'You need to do better at hiding your reaction, *cara mia*. A less scrupulous man would take advantage of it,' he murmured.

With more strength than she'd thought herself capable of, Violet drew away from him, her hands dropping to clench at her sides. The observation stung far deeper than it should've. Made her lash out. 'You think yourself scrupulous? Enlighten me again as to who kidnapped whom?'

The briefest glimpse of regret flashed in his eyes, then he was back to being the imperious Prince who expected everyone to fall in with his wishes, whether they wanted to or not.

'That was different. And necessary.'

'Why?'

Thunder gathered on his brow. 'Besides taking steps to safeguard my child?'

What had happened to him to fuel this raging mistrust? Was it even worth her attempting to find out the reason?

'We agreed on reciprocity, Zak. Are you going back on your word already?'

The gleam in his eyes was almost...approving. Saluting her for turning his words back on him. 'Very well. Ask your questions.'

Given the freedom, she almost feared his answers. Not because they would turn her off him...but because they might *not*. Nevertheless, she couldn't resist. 'When I told you I was pregnant, you reminded me of your half-brother and what his arrival did to your family. But Europe is lit-tered with royal scandals and no one even blinks at them any more. So what am I missing, Zak?'

Dio mio, but she fired with both guns and aimed for the heart, didn't she?

He tensed, anticipating that bolt of anguish. On cue it arrived, accompanied by a heavy dose of bitterness. He considered deflecting her question, but how could he? This truce had been his idea, a way to end the deadlock between them. He couldn't backtrack now.

Hell, perhaps baring himself a little might work to his advantage, just as he'd hoped for and witnessed her genu-ine appreciation for the better qualities of his island dur-ing their tour.

Still, the exercise was…hard.

'Is it really that bad?' she enquired, her voice soft, ooz-ing sympathy he perhaps didn't deserve but couldn't help absorbing regardless. Because he realised that when it came to her, he was extremely selfish. Wanted more and more and *more*.

Everything?

He clenched his gut, denying that horrifyingly damning word that required far too much self-examination. 'Your family isn't without its own…challenges, no?' he stalled, brazenly buying himself time before reopening old wounds of disgrace and betrayal.

Pained shadows flitted across her breathtaking face and fleetingly he regretted his parry.

She stared down at her knotted fingers, then met his gaze. 'No, it isn't, but mine is an open, ugly secret. And before you dig deeper, I'll confess that I've hated every single moment of it. Finding out my parents would do just about anything, even risk bankruptcy, for the sake of so-cial ladder-climbing was…horrifying. Being whispered about, mocked and sometimes openly taunted about a fall from grace and being regarded as scum isn't fun. Neither is being paraded about like a prized heifer at a meat market.'

'No. I don't believe it is,' he found himself answering, for the first time catching a glimpse of what her mother's actions had done to her. He recognised the torment. But he also saw the fight in her. The ferocity it took to stand her ground. Against him. Against the world. Zak couldn't deny that the flame this added to her allure continually drew him.

Her chin lifted, eyes swimming with anguish striking him deeper than he wanted to admit. 'I can't escape my past neither can I disown my parents, but, regardless of what anyone believes, I've no wish to follow in their footsteps. If nothing else, please believe that.'

He believed her. If the past two weeks had achieved anything it was the revelation that she wasn't holding out for more. That, should he feel inclined to grant her passage off this island, Violet would walk away from him without a backward glance, his proposal and enticements and his increasing need to bestow the title of Princess on her be damned.

Again that hollow feeling of dismay threatened to consume him. He ruthlessly stemmed it. Aware that the spotlight was firmly back on him, he gritted his jaw. And bared himself. 'I looked up to him. Perhaps that was my first mistake.' He couldn't contain the deep bitterness that spilled out.

She frowned. 'Your father?'

He nodded. 'He was flawless in my eyes. The embodiment of my every aspiration. I wanted to be just like him. I wasn't going to inherit the throne, but I could walk in his footsteps.' He stopped, the words sounding foolish in his ears.

'No one is flawless, Zak,' she replied gently. 'He may have been larger than life itself to you but he was still human. Nothing more.'

Zak swallowed hard, heat and ice cascading through him at her hushed words. Hadn't he fallen for temptation himself after swearing he never would?

Had he held his father up to stricter standards than were warranted? Idolised him when he should've remembered he was mere flesh and blood? No.

'He was a *king*. He was supposed to have been above reproach. Beyond base flaws—especially flaws that caused harm to his family,' he gritted out.

'You've accepted Jules into your family. Can't you find a way to get past what your father did?'

'No! His affair with Jules's mother wasn't a fleeting thing. It went on for *years*. And while he was busy letting his family down, others were plotting behind his back. He put his kingdom in peril, gave a platform to those who would destabilise the government,' he seethed.

Violet's eyes widened in surprise. 'I…didn't know that.'

His lips twisted. 'Very few people do.'

Silence stretched tight between them. Then she laid a hand on his forearm. He looked into her brilliant blue eyes. Yearned to lose herself in them.

'Do you hate him for that or hate that he died before he could give you the answers you seek? I know I felt…robbed of the need to understand why my father would risk everything just for money.'

Damn this woman! From the very first she'd seen too much, burrowed far deeper than he'd allowed anyone else to go, save perhaps the father he now condemned.

'What does it matter?' he rasped bitterly.

'Because if it's the latter, you'll have to learn to let it go some time, Zak. To forgive and move on before it consumes you. Be the better version of the man your father couldn't be.'

The urge to rail, issue commands, assert his royal will rose fast and furious. But he knew he would be wasting his breath. Violet had no fear of him or his station. If any-thing, she would laugh in his face. So he pursed his lips, even as her words seeped deep into his soul, the truth of it ringing in his ears.

For the first time Zak knew real fear. Because what if he couldn't be a better man? What if Violet and his child found him…lacking?

With a ferocity that would've done his ancestors proud, he cut off the weakening train of thought. He was a *prince*. The blood of warriors ran through his veins. He'd never cowered before anyone. He wasn't about to start now.

'Are we done with this sharing or do you have more questions?'

Violet barely managed to stop herself from gasping at the transformation from vulnerable man to imperious prince. The loss, even more than baring her soul about her past, caught her on the raw. Because she'd glimpsed beneath the power and majesty, seen the real man who, like her, had been let down by his parent. One he'd put on a pedestal.

This was what she'd feared.

That his revelations would end up costing her even more emotionally.

Because even now, watching his stony face, she wanted to wrap her arms around him, lay her head on his chest and just…*be with him*. Be the cushion his hard edges landed on. But he was distancing himself even as she watched, his gaze growing impenetrable as he stared down at her.

Wasn't it wise to do the same?

'You said there hadn't been illegitimacy in your family besides Jules. But what about divorces?'

Grey eyes bored into hers, his attempt to read between the lines clear in his incisive gaze. 'A few, yes.'

Why did that not bring the relief she'd hoped for?

Slowly his face hardened. 'If you're already contemplating the end of a union before it's even begun—'

She forced a laugh. 'Please don't pretend what you proposed is some sort of love match. We both know it was only because I'm pregnant.'

'It's a very powerful reason. One not to be dismissed, as you seem so hell-bent on doing.'

'On our first day here you took pains to spell out what you wanted. Let me tell you what I want. I want the freedom to choose who I spend the rest of my life with. I won't settle for you simply because you happen to be the father of the child I'm carrying.'

A storm brewed in his eyes. '*Settle?* Perhaps you've been blind to the fact that all of Europe and large swathes of the Western world consider me a very big catch indeed.'

'Then they're more than welcome to you!' she responded heatedly, hurt and jealousy and the yearning for the man who'd bared himself to her minutes ago creating a wild, volatile tornado in her heart.

His eyes gleamed and Violet knew something had changed. For one thing, this was the most animated she'd allowed herself to be in his presence for quite some time. And he was savouring his triumph. 'Are you awakened at last, my sweet?'

'Don't call me that, I'm not your anything.'

Keen speculation brimmed in his eyes. 'But you could be, if only—'

'I see sense?' she finished for him. 'Your new offer is to marry you and gain the side benefit of hot sex?'

One sleek thumb brushed over her full bottom lip, a gesture that reeked too boldly of *ownership.* The kind that triggered a shivery response within her. 'I'm glad you acknowledge it will be hot. And, yes, it could be an infinitely pleasurable benefit of our marriage. Think about it.'

'You're forgetting something, Your Highness.'

'What's that?'

She took a decided step back away from temptation. 'Chemistry doesn't last for ever. Or even long enough for the ink to dry on a marriage certificate,' she pointed out. 'Thanks but, no, thanks, I won't base my future on that.'

Seconds ticked by, then Zak dragged his hands through his hair, a tense, self-mocking smile curving his lips. 'A hell of a way to start a truce, hmm?'

She shrugged. 'We seem to bring out the worst in each other, it seems.'

'I wouldn't quite call it that,' he murmured, his voice low and thick.

Alarmed she was about to drown in another torrent of emotional vulnerability, she averted her gaze from the rakish tousle of his hair and the strong bronzed throat that made her fingers itch to caress him.

He glanced at his sleek wristwatch. 'We've done enough for one day, I think. Let's get back to the villa. Dinner will be served in an hour.'

And just like that, the thought that she would be spending some more time with him sent twin pulses of pleasure and fear through her.

Because, more than anything, she wanted another glimpse at the man beneath the stiff royal exterior. Wanted to soothe his fears, share his dreams. Wanted to take her place next to him. Because *that man* was the one she hadn't quite allowed herself to dream about.

But she'd seen him, witnessed a crack in his façade. And as Zak held out his hand to her once more, Violet couldn't help the sensation growing in her heart. Or quieten the voice that whispered that the crack might fracture...perhaps even break apart to reveal his true self...with time and patience.

With love?

CHAPTER NINE

VIOLET REFUSED TO admit that the truce was the reason she took her time with dressing that evening. She was simply sharing an animosity-free meal with Zak.

He was waiting for her in the elegant dining room that opened up into a wide terrace. A sea breeze wafted in, the reminder that she was on a true tropical paradise lingering in the air.

A paradise she hadn't chosen to be on, true, but with their truce in place, she chose to suspend her outrage. Perhaps it was a foolish and slippery slope, but as she watched Zak, clad in dark tailored trousers and white, open-necked shirt, confidently stroll over to her, his gaze taking in her sea-green chiffon dress and returning to her face with latent fire in his eyes, Violet decided to just…go with the flow.

'You look exquisite,' he breathed, his low voice low pulsing with a cadence that trebled her heartbeat.

'I… Thank you.'

His lips curved in a smile as he picked up a frosted glass from the table and held it out to her. 'Here, try this.'

She accepted the offering. 'What is it?'

'A special fruit punch prepared by Geraldine. She swears it works wonders with morning sickness.'

About to ask what conversation had gone on between Zak and his housekeeper regarding her pregnancy, she decided to let it go. He'd lauded their loyalty and discretion on the day of their arrival. It stood to reason that they'd already know that she was pregnant.

She lifted the glass, the umbrella perched on it tickling

her nose as she took a sip. Delicious bursts of coconut underlain with ginger delighted her taste buds. She groaned and took the second sip.

'I take it you like it,' he said, amused.

'Oh, my God, yes, it's amazing.'

His smile widened and that treacherous, giddy sensation inside her expanded. At that exact moment she recalled her throwaway comment earlier this afternoon about the women of Europe being welcome to him.

Violet wanted to blurt out that she hadn't meant it. They weren't welcome to him. Because *she* wanted him. She bit her tongue in time, redirecting her attention to the dining table. Complete with exquisite twin candelabra, fine crystal and sterling silver cutlery, it was the most elaborate setting she'd seen since her arrival.

It was almost as if this evening was different. *Special*.

Furiously wrestling her leaping senses under control, she allowed Zak to guide her to the table.

He refilled her punch glass, poured a white Chablis for himself and sat back as the first course of poached fish and flavoured rice was served.

Registering that Zak was more interested in staring at her than in his own meal, Violet scrambled for a neutral topic. 'What's on the other side of the island?'

Again he smiled, and again her heart tripped with alarming giddiness and the mouth-watering sight of it. God, she really needed to get herself together. She couldn't swoon each time he smiled.

'It's a surprise,' he replied.

'You know all it'll take is a conversation with the staff to have my answer, don't you?'

He sat back and shrugged, unaffected by her harmless threat. 'If you wish to deny yourself the pleasure of an unbiased experience, go ahead.'

Intrigued, she stared at him, his eyes gleaming challengingly at her.

Violet was enjoying this. Far too much. While he wasn't allowing her another glimpse of the man she'd seen this afternoon, she appreciated this more casual side of Zak. Enough to explore it, see where it went?

Temptation swelling inside her, she lifted her glass and, keeping eye contact with him, took a long, deep pull of the tangy drink.

His gaze dropped to her mouth, his eyes darkening dramatically. Tiny flames leapt in her belly and her fingers trembled when she set the glass down. That set the tone for their meal, a pulse-elevating mix of heavy-lidded looks, light conversation and good food.

It took a moment for her to admit the emotion she experienced when their plates were cleared away was regret. It was barely eight, and the thought of spending the rest of the evening alone in her room dimmed her spirits.

'A non-alcoholic nightcap on the beach? Or would you like coffee here?'

He'd barely issued the invitation when she caught a whiff of coffee and her stomach lurched alarmingly. She swallowed hard, fervently praying she wouldn't disgrace herself. 'Definite *no* to the coffee. For the next few weeks at least.'

Zak stared at her with a small frown. With a flick of his hand he summoned the butler. 'Cancel the coffee and inform Geraldine she's not to serve coffee at any meal until further notice.'

'Of course, Your Highness,' Patrick responded, then swiftly exited.

'You didn't need to do that.'

Again he gestured, and the action she used to find so irritating was suddenly the sexiest thing she'd seen.

'Of course I do. Your comfort is of paramount importance.'

Violet scrambled for her good sense before it fled. 'You mean the baby's, of course.'

A weighted emotion crossed his face but was gone the next second. 'You're carrying my child but that doesn't mean your personal well-being isn't also essential.' His gaze dropped to her stomach, stayed for a pulse-racing few seconds. 'I intend to be careful with you both.'

The words burrowed deep, infusing her with warmth and eroding her attempts to guard her vulnerable emotions. She was still struggling when he rose from the table and held out his hand to her.

'A little fresh air will do you good. Hopefully by the time we return the offensive smell will be gone.'

Unable to argue with that, she placed her hand in his. He laced his fingers with hers, immediately setting off tiny fireworks beneath her skin.

Again, Violet decided to let it be.

Beyond the terrace and pristine gardens they went down shallow steps that led to the beach bathed in moonlight. When he tossed his shoes away and urged her to do the same, she didn't object. She was sticking to the spirit of their truce, she told herself.

But gradually it became much more than that.

Heavy, sensual tension lingered in the air, the kind that made her aware of every cell in her body.

When it grew too thick to bear, she frantically cast around for something to dissipate it. 'How long have you owned this place?'

His gaze slanted to her, stayed and lingered over her hair, her jaw, the swell of her bust before he answered. 'Five years. I'd been looking a long time for a place like this and made the owner an offer he didn't refuse.'

'It seems like an it's-been-in-my-family-since-the-dawn-of-time kind of place.'

One corner of his mouth lifted. 'Why would you think that?'

She shrugged. 'Isn't that the way it goes with royalty?'

He gave a low, husky laugh. The sound settled low in her pelvis, heating her up from the inside out. 'Am I being pigeonholed again, Violet?'

'Merely returning the favour,' she parried.

His smile disappeared, and he tugged on her hand to still her. 'Explain.' His voice was terse.

'Isn't that how you see me? In a specific way you won't be swayed from?' She couldn't quite keep the hurt from her voice.

'Several weeks ago, perhaps.'

The unexpected response drew a soft gasp. 'Are you saying that you no longer think I'm scheming to get my hands on your royal billions?' she tossed at him.

He studied her as a scientist would a rare and exotic specimen. 'You may be exceptional in many ways, but I don't think hiding your true character is sustainable in the long run.' He stepped closer, saturating her with his power and might and utter gorgeousness. 'I heard what you said this afternoon, Violet,' he rasped low and deep.

Heard was one thing. But did he believe her?

She wanted to ask. Wanted to lay bare every fear and secret yearning, every hope and fantasy in a way that scared her enough to pull away, attempt to disentangle her fingers from his.

He held her tight as his hand slowly rose, splayed with reverent gentleness on her stomach. Grey eyes gleaming with an emotion she couldn't name, he tugged her close once more. 'We're going to be indefinitely connected by this unique and sacred experience. Let's not default to animosity.'

'I never wanted animosity in the first place.'

His hand shifted, his palm caressing her stomach almost

possessively. 'Good, then let's address something else. This thing between us,' he drawled.

Her mouth dried, her senses jumping as she fought her own yearnings. 'What are you talking about?'

His free hand slid beneath her thick braid to grip her tighter. He pulled her closer, rested his forehead against hers. 'You're like a fever in my blood, Violet. I crave you beneath me, satisfying your every need, your beautiful body bare to my every whim.'

A deeper shiver attacked her, unravelling her from head to toe. Zak didn't miss her reaction, and smiled in pure, arrogant male satisfaction at her response to his words.

'I… I don't…'

He grazed his thumb over her lips, dredging another tremble from her soul. 'Before you deny us, think for a moment, my sweet, of how much better this truce could be if you can have me, without guilt or hesitation, anytime and anywhere you want,' he urged thickly. His voice oozed pure temptation, so much carnal promise Violet could barely keep her body upright.

Seven days of untold pleasure.

The thought that with one move he'd imprisoned her and with the other he was granting her sexual freedom was almost too much to wrap her head around.

His fierce intelligence had always astounded her, but Zak was demonstrating how he held the world effortlessly in the palm of his hand.

Even the acknowledgement that he'd guided her into the middle of this maelstrom, that she would most likely be annihilated before the tempest was over, wasn't enough to compel her back from the dizzying edge his words had propelled her to.

Seven days of indulging her every fantasy.

And then what?

She couldn't lose sight of his ultimate purpose. Everything he was doing was for his child. Well, except maybe the urge to scratch this particular itch.

But...it was the same craving she was experiencing. And wasn't this the perfect opportunity to crack that hardened emotional shell? Heal him even as she attempted to heal herself?

Her insides shook at the gleaming possibility of what could be.

His fingers drifted from her nape to her jaw, caressed her cheek as he tilted her head to meet his. 'Everything you desire will be yours,' he vowed thickly.

Did that include his heart?

She shook her head to dissipate the sudden, explosive yearning but it piled higher, dug deeper, frightening her with the strength of it. But even as she fought, she knew she was going to accept Zak's proposition.

The chance for something *more* was too tempting.

Lifting a trembling hand, she glided it over his wrist, laid over her cheek, and pressed his touch deeper into her skin.

Flames leapt in his eyes but he remained a solid, desperate foot away from her. 'Do you agree, Violet?'

'What do you think?'

'I think I want the pleasure of hearing you say yes,' he answered, a sensual edge rimming his voice.

Her heart banged against her ribs. 'Yes, I agree.'

With a thick groan, he freed their connecting fingers, placed his palm in the small of her back, and tugged her into his body.

Violet experienced a stunning new level of sensuality as his tongue probed raw and deep, with an edge of possessiveness that snatched the breath from her lungs. With effortless ease, he lifted her, plastered her body against his in a shameless demonstration of his physical prowess that had her groaning and clinging to him.

When he urged her legs around his waist, Violet gladly

complied, her sense swimming when the action imprinted his thick potent manhood against her heated core.

They both groaned, their breaths growing ragged as they strained together, right there on his perfect beach.

'I want to lay you here on the sand, share you with the moonlight as I bury myself deep inside you. But not tonight. Tonight I will take you in my bed.'

Zak was already moving, only one destination in mind as he strode with gritted-jaw purpose back to the villa.

Violet didn't take a breath until the doors of his master suite slammed behind them. Then the reality of what she'd agreed threatened to overwhelm her. As if he knew her depths of her emotion, Zak placed a gentle kiss on her lips.

Eyes locked on hers, he walked over to the wide, inviting bed and eased her to her feet. 'Turn around,' he instructed gruffly.

Glad for the brief reprieve of not staring at his overwhelming perfection, she obliged him. But the brush of his hand at her nape, the sound of him lowering her zipper created a whole new set of sizzling anticipation.

The dress pooled at her feet, and he inhaled sharply. 'Once again I find you without a bra. Is it your intention to torture me at every turn?'

She cast a glance over her shoulder. 'How is this torture?'

'Because now I'll spend far too much time obsessing over your state of undress beneath your clothes,' he griped.

Female satisfaction curled through her. 'Oh.'

His teeth bared in a smile that was near feral enough to make her toes curl into the carpet, Zak stepped forward, curling one large hand over her bottom. Her breath hitched in her throat as he squeezed her bottom and one breast at the same time.

'It's going to drive me insane, you know that, don't you?'

Violet groaned, the idea of Zak thinking about her in

that way not an unpleasant one. In fact, it was so pleasing she smiled.

'Ah, there it is again, that sassy little acknowledgement of your power. Are you ready to experience mine now, my sweet?'

He plucked one nipple, squeezed and tormented that tight little bud until her body was a column of fire racked with deep, carnal shivers.

Her gasps only spurred him on, his body bowing over hers as he stoked her pleasure with his other hand.

She moaned his name again as he lightly bit the sensitive skin beneath her ear. Expertly manipulating those three little points of sensation was all it took for Violet to tumble over the edge, free-falling into bliss so acute, a wild scream erupted from her throat.

When she came to, her upper body was draped over the side of the bed, Zak's arm around her waist holding up as he dragged her panties down her legs.

'I've dreamt of taking you like this,' he rasped, his voice barely discernible through the miasma of lust. 'Do you want this, Principessa?'

'Please,' she begged.

He gave a gruff exhalation, then came the sound of him impatiently disrobing.

One hand caressed her from nape to spine, then with a firm grip on her waist Zak thrust deep into her liquid core.

Pleasure lit up her spine, making Violet toss her head as he stroked inside her.

'*Dio mio*, you're so beautiful. Exceptional.' Words tumbled from his lips, alternately in English and Montegovan, every time driving her closer to another peak of wonder that robbed her of the ability to breathe.

All she could do was grip the sheets, her cries urging him on until with a soul-deep scream she gave herself over to deeper, more intense bliss.

Zak followed close behind, wrapping his body around hers and holding her tight as his guttural shouts echoed alongside hers, filling the room with the ferocity of their pleasure.

He held on tight to her as she floated, weightless, through her climax. When they were both spent, he eased her back onto the bed before joining her and draping her over his body.

Violet's heart dipped alarmingly when he drifted soft kisses over her face and tucked her head beneath his chin. It was a world removed from the aftermath of their coming together in Tanzania. So...special that Violet didn't even want to breathe, lest the moment be ruined.

'You're deafening me with how hard you're thinking, *carissima*.' He caught his finger beneath her chin and lifted her gaze to his. 'Don't tie yourself in knots over this.'

'Fine, then distract me,' she said.

It was like offering the Big Bad Wolf a feast. Pure male anticipation dripped from his blinding smile. 'Oh, the things I have in mind for you...' He kissed her deep and long, and then reluctantly pulled back. 'But for now it would please me if you rested.'

Almost as if her body was designed to obey his every command, a pleasant sort of weariness swept over her. And with her arm wrapped tight over his waist she slept.

While she hadn't quite doubted his words, Violet had no frame of reference for what Zak meant. She could only bear slack-jawed witness to both his sexual prowess and the sheer depth of his intelligence over the next seven days.

By specific instruction, or simply because they were trained that well, the staff kept a discreet distance as Zak introduced her to sensual pleasure all over his villa.

And they talked. Politics, diplomacy and her favourite

subject—conservation. Deep, illuminating conversation that challenged and enlightened.

While he was reluctant to revisit the subject of his father, she gleaned that he adored his mother, perhaps even appreciated her more for her strength in the face of scandal and betrayal.

It was in the aftermath of one such exchange that a kernel of apprehension sprouted. Because it was basking in the spotlight of his full attention, revelling in another heated debate while he caressed her body, and his growing reluctance to leave her side for any length of time that made Violet start to fear for her heart.

In those moments her yearning for him bloomed, threatened to scatter wild and free. To open her most secret emotions to this god of a man with almost overbearing intelligence and faultless pedigree.

The man who leaned attentively closer when she made a point, who challenged her opinion and nodded with appreciation when she succinctly delivered it. Who held her in his arms while she pretended to sleep, the fear that she was losing herself in him leaving her wide awake and terrified. Because she was right, after all. The man beneath the princely surface was the man she wanted for herself. The father she craved for her child.

So it was with mingled relief and trepidation that she opened her eyes on the seventh day since their little tryst and truce began. She struggled not to read anything into the fact that it was the only day she'd woken alone in all that time.

Their lovemaking had been even more intense the night before, the unspoken knowledge that this was their last night together driving the need to extract the most from their last encounter. She'd lost count of how many times she'd shattered with ultimate bliss, had been boneless when Zak had lowered them both into a soothing bath, had washed and dried her body before placing her back in his bed.

The conflicting thoughts stayed with her as she readied herself for breakfast. Dressed in a knee-length yellow wraparound dress, she sat at her dressing table, her fingers tight around her hairbrush.

Zak hadn't asked her to marry him at any point in the last seven days and, perversely, the absence of it had only made her obsess over it.

Would marriage to him be so bad?

He was a royal with billions at his disposal, but he was as committed to conservation and preservation as she was. Could they make a marriage work based on common interests and amazing sex alone or was she deluding herself?

What about her mother?

Margot had gone suspiciously silent in the last few days. The tabloids had been equally silent on her mother's activities, an unusual occurrence since Margot lived for the society pages. Unease slid down Violet's spine as she set the brush down and left the room.

She'd have to face her mother sooner or later. Deliver news of the pregnancy. And then what? Tell her that she'd turned down Zak's proposal or that she'd agreed?

Her heart flipped over. Was she really considering saying yes? To seeing him every day, to sharing his bed, connecting with someone who shared her professional passion?

What about love? The suspicion that ultimately this was only about the child she carried?

She froze as she neared the terrace. Could she marry Zak knowing she was second best behind his need to claim his child? Could she live with that?

Yes, her inner voice urged, even while her spirits dipped.

Could they build on that too, find their way to emotional fulfilment the way they already enjoyed sex and conversation?

She ignored the widening dismay that mocked her scrambled, pathetic excuses. Either she was going into this with her eyes wide open to the fact that Zak didn't see her as anything other than the womb carrying his child and the woman warming his bed, or this threatening heartache would flatten her harder the—

'Do you intend to linger in the doorway all day, *cara*?'

She jumped at the sound of his deep voice and despite the misgivings eating her alive stepped outside, her gaze magnetically drawn to where he sat, resplendent in the sunlight. She went hot all over again not at all surprised when her heart slammed against her ribs at the sight of him.

The thought of losing him sent an acute chill through her, and Violet knew she couldn't turn her back on whatever Zak's proposal entailed.

'What's wrong?'

The sharp enquiry was edged with the fierce determination in his eyes. Her breath stalled, her tongue clinging to the words she wanted to utter. Registering that his edginess had been present when he'd swept her off to bed last night, that she'd been too caught up to heed the look, never mind uncover what it meant, sent another wave of anxiety over her.

Dragging in a steadying breath, she approached and sat down. 'Zak, we need to talk.'

Shadows sharpened his features as he raised a laconic eyebrow at her. 'Do we?'

She slicked her tongue over her lower lip, the enormity of the step she was about to take consuming her whole. 'You know we do.'

Stormy eyes held hers for another ferocious second before he waved at the table. 'Geraldine has prepared everything you like. Don't let it go to waste.'

Suspicion that he was avoiding the subject jangled her nerves even more. She should be grateful for the brief reprieve to consider her decision. But with each morsel she swallowed, the giddiness grew, the urge to blurt that *Yes, I'll marry you*, even entertain that very male satisfaction at finally extracting the answer he wanted, suffusing her.

She thought of what would come after, the many nights and days she would spend with Zak, welcoming their child into the world, nurturing him or her…

Her hand shook with sheer elation, a world removed from the initial dismay she'd felt minutes ago. Setting her teacup down before it spilled, she laced her fingers in her lap and cleared her throat. 'It's been seven days, Zak—'

'Technically, it hasn't. Label me pedantic but we have until mid-afternoon before our time is truly up.'

She couldn't wait that long. She couldn't wait another *minute*. 'Fine, but I think you should know I'm…considering—'

The butler's diplomatic throat-clearing interrupted her.

'What it is?' Zak asked, his eyes narrowed on her face, cataloguing the nerves eating her alive.

'My apologies for the interruption, Your Highness, but His Majesty, your brother, is on the phone for you.'

He rose. 'I have to take it. Excuse me, Violet.'

'But—'

'I don't think it's a good idea to keep the King waiting, do you?' he said drily.

And yet as he walked away, she suspected he would've done exactly that if it'd suited him.

The real possibility that he'd changed his mind siphoned every scrap of joy she'd managed to fool herself into believing she would enjoy by agreeing to marry him.

She finished breakfast, eating more for sustenance than enjoyment. As if to match her mood, stormclouds rolled fast and frantic over the horizon, throwing dark shadows over the villa within minutes.

Torn between awaiting Zak's return and retreating, she

lingered until heavy raindrops began to hammer the pave-stones. Then, restless, anxious and more than a little hor-rified at the sheer depths of a loss she hadn't even suffered yet, she went up to her suite and opened her laptop.

There was still no word from her mother but her boss back in the UK had emailed, asking for a tentative date for her return.

The need to inform Zak of her decision resurged, pro-pelling her from the room. As she'd done so many times since her arrival, she entered his domain via the library, a habit that drew a small smile.

The sound of Zak's deep voice stopped her short. She didn't want to interrupt his conversation with his brother. Deciding to wait rather than return to her suite, Violet froze as a painfully familiar voice answered Zak's crisp query via speakerphone.

Zak was talking to her mother?

She barely registered moving closer to the study door, pressing her ear against the cool wood. The dulcet tones that announced her mother's excitement contained another much-too-familiar pitch, one that spelled absolute triumph, a coup she couldn't wait to crow about. A chill swept over her skin, seeping ice into Violet's soul. Decades of shame lashed her as her mother continued, 'You have my word, Zak. The interview will be tasteful and any that follow will be arranged in consultation with your people.'

'And the nondisclosure agreement?'

Violet pressed her fist to her mouth to prevent an an-guished gasp from escaping.

'My lawyer looked it over yesterday and all is well. Your lawyers should have the signed copies by now. But it really wasn't necessary. You're going to be family soon enough,' her mother gushed, 'and you've already been so generous, paying off my debts and gifting me a house in Montegova for when my grandchild arrives. I should be offended that you'd even feel the need for a non-disclosure agreement.' She laughed off the insult.

Violet couldn't see it but well imagined Zak's arrogant shrug. 'I'm sure your sensibilities will recover from my need to ensure no loopholes are left in securing what's mine.'

Violet's soul shrivelled to dust.

'Of course,' Margot gushed even more. 'The crew is arriving shortly. May I be excused?'

'You may,' Zach answered, his voice containing that edge Violet had heard at the breakfast table. 'I look forward to seeing the outcome.'

'You won't be disappointed, Your Highness.'

Her mother's voice was cut off abruptly, leaving only the sound of the blood rushing through Violet's ears as the ominous death knell of the foolish dreams she'd harboured.

She stumbled back from the door, glad for the Aubusson rug that hid her footfalls, even while she prayed she wouldn't be discovered, granting Zak the excuse to keep her here, devise another cold, calculated strategy to claim his child.

She didn't take a breath until she reached the kitchen.

Geraldine took one look at her and went into mother hen mode, the exact reaction she wanted.

'I'm not feeling great. I think the storm disturbed me more than I thought,' Violet said.

'Oh, don't worry, miss. They tend to pass quickly here.'

Violet nodded abstractly. 'I'm going to lie down. Can you make sure I'm not disturbed by anyone, including Zak?'

The housekeeper frowned but nodded. 'Of course, miss.'

She fled, feeling a twinge of guilt at using her pregnancy as an excuse. A sob clogged her throat as she hurried up the steps. She held it in until she reached her suite.

Then the torrent came.

He'd used the truce to pull the wool over her eyes, while

orchestrating her mother's co-operation with financial incentives and the limelight Margot adored so much. He'd made Violet believe they had a foundation to build a relationship on. And she'd fallen wholesale for the illusion. Given her body, soul, mind and one vital part she desperately feared would never be reclaimed.

She'd given Zak Montegova her heart.

And he'd shattered it.

CHAPTER TEN

VIOLET FEARED SHE would never be whole again.

But gluing her shattered pieces together would have to come later. Right now, she was still trapped on this island, her every vulnerability exposed.

She pulled herself up in bed, her jaw clenching tight. He may have imprisoned her, but hadn't she turned the tables on him for two weeks? She scrubbed at her eyes, blinking when further tears threatened. All she needed was to stage the performance of a lifetime once again, and finally convince him that she would co-operate.

Her heart screamed with agony, strenuously fighting the thought of being separated from the owner, who had no regard for it. Fists clenched tight, she rehearsed her role, acted out every imaginable outcome in her head.

Rising, she entered the bathroom, washed away all traces of tears and touched up the blotchiness with make-up.

The sooner she confronted Zak, the sooner she would gain her freedom.

The gown she wore to Remi's wedding had been dry-cleaned. Matching shoes located, she hurriedly dressed and retrieved her weekend bag. She exited, denying herself one last look at the room. The staccato echo of her heels fell in tandem with her racing heart as she approached the hallway leading to Zak's study.

Her heart lurched when the door was wrenched open.

Zak stood framed in the doorway. '*Cara*, I was told you weren't feeling—' He stopped, his expression morphing from false concern to shock to fury when he took in her attire and the case in her hand. 'What the hell do you think you're doing?' he demanded.

'What does it look like? I'm leaving.'

For a fraction of time she fooled herself into thinking she glimpsed utter bleakness in his eyes. Then his arrogant head reared up, his gaze icing over. 'What happened to talking?'

'I think we've said everything that needs saying.'

He jerked away from the doorway, bringing that deceptive, irresistible magnificence one step closer. 'Violet—'

She stopped him with a dismissive flick of her hand, silently congratulating herself for emulating his imperious gesture. 'There's no point rehashing this all over again, Zak. As you said last week, it's grown boring and tedious.'

Aquiline nostrils flared. 'This has gone infinite ways beyond that and you know it.'

'All I know is that you're holding me here against my will. Your time's up, Zak. Let's end this now before any of this comes back to bite you.' He opened his mouth but again she stopped him. 'Think of the scandal that you're courting by perpetuating this farce, and let's be sensible about it.'

Eyes narrowed, his strong jaw worked as he stared at her with a ferocity that nearly unseated her performance. 'You wanted to talk to me at breakfast. Was this what you intended to say?' he asked, his voice a blade of ice.

She pretended to frown. 'Possibly. I forget now. Blame my hormones.' Again she sent a tiny plea for forgiveness to her baby. 'It's inconsequential now.'

Laser beam eyes probed her. 'What the hell is going on here, Violet? What exactly are you trying to achieve with this performance?'

Terror struck at the threat of discovery. Somehow, she dredged up a scornful laugh. 'You keep saying it's a performance. Is it really so hard to accept that I've had enough of this place? Enough of you?'

His face grew tight, the skin surrounding his lips whitening. Still he came at her, as if he wanted to test her determination up close.

Violet stood her ground, barely holding it together when every cell in her body wanted to retreat from the overwhelming potency of him. She didn't even dare breathe for fear that his addictive scent would demolish her. She raised her chin a fraction higher and met his gaze. 'You have no choice, Zak. You gave me your word. Now let me go.'

For the longest time he didn't respond. His gaze blazed with fury, but Violet caught another emotion in the grey depths. Uncertainty. A hint of vulnerability.

But soon they evaporated as his gaze dropped with sizzling intent to her belly. To the hint of a curve where their child grew. 'You won't get very far with what's mine, Violet,' he vowed.

Her heart lurched at the throb of deep possession in his voice, but it was nothing compared to the leap of her senses at the thought that leaving here today wouldn't quite be the last time she encountered Zak. They would be tied together for ever by their child.

But at what cost? Her sanity? This deep craving she knew in her bones was more than lust? More than simple enthralment with every single thing about him?

It would shatter her completely. She knew that too in her bones. 'I had a feeling you would say that. Expect a letter from my solicitors in the next week or so.'

He inhaled sharply. 'Are you sure you wish to engage in legal battles with me?' he enquired, his tone deadly.

'Of course not. I expect a *civil* discourse between us concerning this baby. It's up to you if you wish to turn it into a battle.'

He shook his head, as if he couldn't quite grasp her response.

Violet wanted to laugh but she daren't, fearing she'd

most likely dissolve into more sobs. She'd cried enough already.

His face turned into a cold mask. 'You should really reconsider. You don't know what you're inviting on yourself with this course of action.'

'I have. You may have wealth, but I have the power and I suspect you won't want to drag your brother and his sparkling new reign through the dirt, all in the name of taking my child away from me. Try it and I'll tell the world everything you've done to me in the last three weeks.'

Stark shock mingled with the fury. 'How did I fool myself into thinking you were different?' he rasped.

Violet allowed herself a small, stiff smile and no more. 'Go easy on yourself, Zak. After all, I fooled myself into thinking the very same of you.'

He stiffened with rigid affront, thunderclouds rolling over his face as he stared at her.

Unable to stand it any longer, she pivoted away from him.

'I'm happy to leave by speedboat if that gets me off this island quicker. I'll be in the living room when it's ready to leave. Goodbye, Zak.'

He didn't respond. And with every step she took away from him, Violet felt his ferocious gaze boring into her skin. She prayed that he wouldn't follow even as her shockingly traitorous heart prayed he would.

When he didn't…when all she received was a message from the butler to say his plane would arrive in three hours to take her off the island, she cursed the silent, defiant tears that poured out of her broken heart.

Zak stood at his study window, eyes fixed on the plane poised at the start of the runway. The intermittent thunderstorms that had pummelled the villa throughout the day had finally receded and his pilot had been cleared for take-off.

His fingers clenched hard, shooting pain up his arms. He ignored it, the strain of remaining in control demanding every ounce of his willpower.

He couldn't believe he'd spent the past week with an illusion. That Violet had taken exactly she'd wanted and then left him.

What he had offered her, the inner voice insisted.

He snarled under his breath, wishing with every bone in his body that he could move from the window, wrench his gaze from the plane taking her away from him.

She never belonged to you.

He'd taken steps to protect his family, his child, and it'd backfired. That was all.

No, that wasn't all. At this exact moment she was taking his heart away from him and he didn't mean the child she carried.

Her beautiful smile.

Her laughter.

Her intelligence, vitality and passion.

Everything he hadn't known was essential to him until the moment he'd seen her in that blasted gown, clutching that godforsaken weekend bag. She'd walked away with everything he feared he would need to be able to breathe again.

Because somewhere between New York and Tanzania and the Caribbean, he'd fallen in love with Violet Barringhall. And once again he'd experienced the true depths of betrayal and shattered dreams.

But…had she really betrayed him?

She'd promised him nothing save the pleasure of the body she'd given selflessly.

In his supreme arrogance he'd believed he could sway her with his royal pedigree and the title of Princess, when the only thing that brought her truly alive was her work.

The irony of it, he reflected bitterly, that he'd thrown a

proposal at the feet of the only woman who would reject him so resoundingly. What did Violet want that he lacked? The question echoed in his mind as he watched the plane gather speed.

Fingers unclenched, he braced them against the cool glass window, a deep rumble erupting from his chest, gaining momentum as the plane's engines grew louder, forcefully announcing that he'd failed, that he'd gambled and lost, his very heart torn from his chest.

The pain grew. Unable to contain it, Zak released it in a loud bellow, both hands clenching in his hair as the aircraft lifted into the air and banked steeply. Its sleek wings caught the sunlight, delivering a mocking wink before righting itself again.

He barely registered stumbling to his desk, blinded by the overwhelming sense of loss hollowing his insides. Every sinew strained for action, specifically one that involved calling his pilot, ordering the plane back to the island. But what Violet didn't know was that all his excuses for his actions were no longer valid.

His general had finally located the rebels.

And with Remi's own news this morning that his new wife was pregnant, and a public announcement was imminent, any immediate threat to Montegova and his family were effectively neutralised.

By ordering Violet back, wasn't he compounding his sins by acting as his bloodthirsty ancestors had in centuries past? The simple truth was that she didn't want him. Had no interest in his royal pedigree, his wealth...*nothing*.

Accepting the stark truth took several swigs from his favourite vintage cognac. But an hour later Zak was still clear-eyed, his pain just as all-consuming. With a grimace, he tossed the mostly full bottle aside. He'd suffered through his father's betrayal, through the scandal of Jules's arrival in their lives, had put out several different fires in the name of family since then.

He would handle this too.

First thing tomorrow he'd instruct his lawyers to begin the process of claiming his child.

And you're happy with her hating you even more than she does now?

He growled at the inner voice. It persisted, his conscience…an almost evangelic need to make Violet happy despite her rejection of him forcing him to reconsider that action.

Desperate, he mentally replayed their last conversation at the breakfast table.

'Zach, I think you should know I'm considering…'

His heart leapt, defying his usual circumspection and cynicism. Considering what? Accepting his proposal?

Had he shut her off too soon, fearing the very rejection she'd delivered such a short time later? He dragged frantic fingers through his hair. Had he destroyed any chance of making her his? *Dio mio…* Or becoming hers?

He reached for the phone, this time to summon his pilot to turn the plane around for a completely different reason. To plead for the woman he loved.

Instead, the phone rang.

Wild hope flaring in his heart, he picked it up.

Margot Barringhall's panicked voice cut through his greeting. 'Zak… Your Highness, we have a problem.'

Ice doused his veins. 'What is it?'

'I don't know how it happened but… Violet just called me. I… She knows about you paying off my debts, about the house in Montegova… She knows everything—'

His vision blurred for a moment, that wild hope dying a swift, merciless death. 'How?' Even as the hoarse demand erupted from his throat, he knew.

She'd overheard him.

Heard and had rightly condemned him for his actions. Dread spiralled through him. 'Did you explain things to her?'

'No... I couldn't, could I? I signed the NDA—'

Zak bit back a snarl, the thought that she would leave her daughter to suffer just so she wouldn't lose out financially making him want to lash out.

But he couldn't. The blame was his alone. He'd acted without consulting her, taken steps to mitigate circumstances that might never have arisen. For all he knew, Margot Barringhall could've surprised him the way her daughter had already stunned him.

But hard lessons that'd shaped his life had urged him to react in the only way he knew how. He refocused as Margot's undisguised panic drilled into his skull.

'She's threatening to disown me, Zak. She wants nothing to do with me. I might never meet my grandchild. I... You need to do something. *Please*. I can't lose her.'

Zak hung up, his skin ashen, his mouth a thin white line. Margot Barringhall may have discovered her humanity too late to salvage her relationship with her daughter. And if Violet was threatening to disown her own mother, what chance did he have with her?

He'd faced down tyrants and dictators in his time in the military, thwarted threats against his family. Why did the thought of dealing with one woman terrify him?

Because she wasn't just any woman.

She was the woman he loved.

Violet focused the fragments of attention she could summon on the wide screen that tracked the plane's flight path to London. As if keeping it in sight would dull the pain rippling through her veins. She'd prayed she'd got it wrong, that she'd misinterpreted Zak's conversation. But her mother's caginess and eventual confession that her NDA forbade her from discussing her agreement with Zak had killed any last dregs of hope.

Seven short hours.

Then she could find a quiet hotel to hide away in. Having given up the flat she'd shared with Sage after her twin's departure and her own temporary relocation to New York, Violet had nowhere to go save the house she'd grown up in, and she had no intention of returning to Barringhall. It hadn't felt like home in a long time anyway. Knowing the very roof over her head was paid for with greed and shameless money-grabbing antics had soured it for her a long time ago.

She would give herself a few days, then start flat-and job-hunting. She had a baby coming. As much as she wanted to wallow in misery she—

She sucked in a breath as the plane banked sharply to the left. That in itself wasn't unusual, but the onscreen map flickering off for a moment before returning with a different destination was what stopped her breath completely.

He wouldn't dare!

Please, God, let him not do this. Violet didn't think she could stand it. The moment the plane righted itself, she grabbed the phone that handily announced its connection with the pilot.

He answered on the first ring. 'My apologies, Lady Barringhall, I was about to step out and apprise you of the flight plan change.'

'Tell me we're not returning to the island?'

'Ah… I'm afraid I can't.' It didn't help that he sounded genuinely regretful.

It didn't help that her heart leapt for a wild, shameful moment before crashing harder than before. It didn't help that when they landed back on the island an hour later, Zak stood on the tarmac, uncaring that his hair was wildly tousled by the turbulent air or that the all-white linen shirt and trousers only highlighted his perfection.

But she *could* help staying in her seat long after the pilot disembarked with his crew.

And she remained seated, her heart in her throat, as Zak watched her through the window until his staff drove away. Only then did he mount the stairs into the plane.

It'd only been a few hours since she'd seen him, but it felt like a lifetime had passed. He still looked devilishly breathtaking.

Formidable. Imperious. Calculating as he paused at the front of the plane, stormcloud eyes devouring her. After an age he turned to the door and pressed a series of buttons. In under a minute they were sealed in.

Panic flared through her but she fought to keep it from showing. 'I'm starting to think you have a bondage fetish, Your Highness. Shall I add that to the list of your sins?'

He sauntered down the aisle, his watchful gaze unwavering. Expecting him to take the seat opposite, Violet let out a soft gasp when he sank to his knees in front of her. 'Tell me what you intended to say at breakfast this morning, Violet.'

'I told you, I don't remember—'

He leaned forward, his throat moving convulsively. 'Please, *carissima*. Tell me,' he implored.

'Why?' she whispered.

His hands suddenly gripped hers, their fine tremor triggering an earthquake inside her. 'Because I suspect I made a very terrible mistake in not delaying taking my brother's call.'

The air left her lungs but she fought against the tendrils of hope teasing her shattered emotions. 'Did Remi really call?'

He frowned, then nodded. 'Of course. He called to tell me I'm to become an uncle. Why would you think otherwise?'

She held his gaze without answering, her eyes widening when sharp regret darkened his eyes. 'You think I deceived you,' he declared.

'I spoke to my mother, Zak. And I heard you this morning.'

'I know you did. She called to inform me.'

She gasped, pain stabbing her heart. 'So what is this? Why bring me back here?'

'Because I'm learning that my way of doing things won't always reap the results I want.'

'You think?'

His eyes glinted, his gaze dropping to her mouth before his expression tightened. 'The moment you informed me you were carrying our child, very little else ceased to matter except ensuring your safety and welfare.'

She shook her head. 'Don't wrap it up in concern for me. You wanted me out of the way, hidden away like some dirty little secret—'

'Hidden away, yes, but not like a secret.' His jaw gritted for a moment before he continued. 'My other reasons still apply but…my father's generals, men he trusted, tried to target the throne within hours of his death. Montegova was birthed through war and bloodshed. My people can be a little…bloodthirsty. Luckily, I had a network of trusted men who don't believe in senseless violence and tyranny.'

'Is that why you've kept an eye on the current general?'

He nodded. 'I vowed that we wouldn't get caught with our guard down ever again. That included removing you from any possible line of attack.'

She gasped. 'Why didn't you tell me?'

'I was going to, eventually. But…this last week was special and I selfishly wanted to hang onto it.' She was busy catching her breath when he added, 'And then I was made aware of your mother's activities.'

Her heart dropped. 'My mother?'

His lips firmed. 'She was pitting tabloids against each other, hoping to start a bidding war on a story about you. And me.'

A hot wave of shame engulfed her. But even through it, bitterness at his actions remained. 'And so you bought her off.'

'I offered her a different...better alternative.'

'An alternative?'

'A chance to celebrate her coming grandchild, rather than capitalise financially on the occasion. An interview with a journalist of my choice, to be aired with your strict approval once the baby was born and once you'd vetted every word. In return, I offered to settle her debts.'

'What else did you do? Tell her to pressure me to marry you? To keep all of this from her own daughter under threat of persecution from your non-disclosure agreement?'

His lips firmed, but he didn't deny any of it. 'Perhaps I was delusional but I didn't want to entertain the thought that this week would end with you refusing to marry me. *Dio mio*, the possibility of you leaving me, despite everything I'd done...' He shook his head. 'I'm used to winning, Violet. To being in control.'

'Because everyone around you expects it? Don't you know that's unrealistic?'

'If I can't hold myself accountable, how can I expect others to be?'

She frowned, her heart lurching at the pain in his voice. 'Are you talking about your father again?'

Cold bleakness filled his eyes before they dropped to the hands clutching hers. 'I wasted years believing he could walk on water. I even excused him when he didn't display much affection, when he seemed especially harsh.' He shrugged. 'Trying to live with that lie has been...hard.'

She didn't realise she'd twisted her fingers to entwine

with his until he lifted hers to kiss her knuckles. 'He shattered your trust, but not everyone is like that.'

'Perhaps it was my misfortune to encounter those who reinforced that belief.'

'Am I lumped with that lot?'

Her heart leapt when he immediately shook his head. 'Not you, Violet. You turned my suspicions inside out. *Dio*, you turned me inside out,' he rasped fervently. 'Your passion. Your beauty. Your spirit, challenging me at every turn. I was addicted to you long before I had you in Tanzania.'

Her heart banged against her ribs. 'What…what are you saying, Zak?'

'That telling me about the baby was the perfect strategy I used to attempt to bind you to me. I could've picked anywhere in the world to bring you but I picked this island because I wanted to show you what we had in common. What we could achieve together.'

'I saw,' she murmured, almost too afraid to hope. 'I saw and I yearned for it. So much it frightened me.'

He froze. 'Violet?' Her name was a thick, husky imploration.

She swayed towards him. 'Yes, Zak.'

'Tell me what you meant to say this morning,' he repeated.

'Why?'

Piercing eyes probed hers, his intentions blazing ferociously. 'Because I love you. I will give my life to protect you and our child. I regret taking your choices away. Because I'm obsessed with you, with your passion. With your body. With your grace. With the humbling thought that you're the one carrying my child, giving me the opportunity to be the kind of father I wanted mine to be.'

The depth of feeling in his voice shook her to the core. 'Zak…'

'Most of all, I want to do everything in my power to

make you the happiest woman alive if it's your intention to stay or move mountains to earn your love at some point in the future.'

'So you're not going to sic your lawyers on me?' she teased.

'They're at the ready to agree to your every stipulation.'

'*Carte blanche*? Really?'

A humbled look crossed his face, but since Zak was who he was, it didn't linger for long. 'I trust you, Violet. I've seen into your heart. I know you won't keep my child from me simply to make us both suffer.'

Perhaps it was that final endorsement. Perhaps it was the pregnancy hormones. With a tearful gasp, she leaned into him until their noses brushed, until she was breathing his essence into herself, filling every cracked corner of her heart with him, letting him make her whole again.

'Zak?'

'*Si, cara?*' he replied thickly, his gaze shifting from her eyes to her mouth.

'I was going to say yes. Because I love and adore you too. Because I want to wear that ring you kept threatening me with. Because I want to be not just the Principessa on paper but the queen of your heart. Because I want half a dozen babies, and you seem enthusiastic enough to fulfil that particular fantasy.'

He caught her in his arms and laid her on the plush carpet in the aisle. 'I don't know, *amore*, it's been a whole twelve hours since I last had you. I could be rusty, you know.'

She slid her arms around his neck. 'Then we'd better find out, yes?'

'Indeed, *mi amore*,' he breathed as he divested her of her clothes. 'With my love, my soul, and my everlasting pleasure.'

* * * * *

LET'S TALK

Romance

For exclusive extracts, competitions
and special offers, find us online:

f facebook.com/millsandboon

⊙ @millsandboonuk

🐦 @millsandboon

Or get in touch on 0844 844 1351*

For all the latest titles coming soon,
visit millsandboon.co.uk/nextmonth